W9-DBN-054

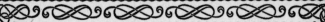

THREE SIRENS CLASSICS

Uniform with this set

*The best selected works of the following list
of great authors are available in six volume
de luxe sets, issued by the Three Sirens Press*

DICKENS

GEORGE ELIOT

EMERSON & PLATO

HAWTHORNE

LAMB

SMOLLETT

FIELDING

DE MAUPASSANT

KIPLING

STEVENSON

POE

THREE SIRENS PRESS
104 FIFTH AVENUE, NEW YORK

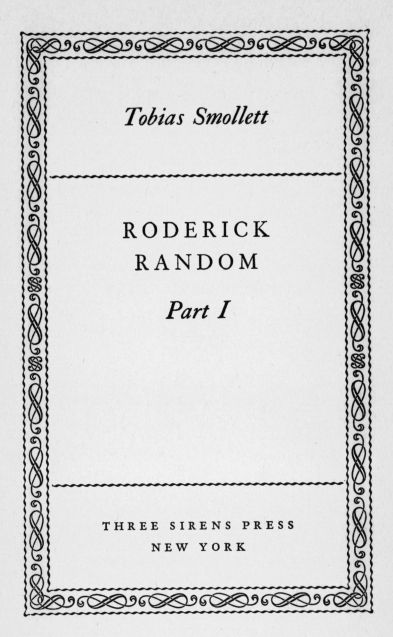

Tobias Smollett

RODERICK
RANDOM

Part I

THREE SIRENS PRESS
NEW YORK

PR
3694
R6

PRINTED IN THE UNITED STATES OF AMERICA
BY J. J. LITTLE AND IVES COMPANY, NEW YORK

S 23.63
S 7r
23793

PZ
3
S6.665
R6

THE PREFACE

OF all kinds of satire, there is none so entertaining and universally improving, as that which is introduced, as it were, occasionally, in the course of an interesting story, which brings every incident home to life; and, by representing familiar scenes in an uncommon and amusing point of view, invests them with all the graces of novelty, while nature is appealed to in every particular.

The reader gratifies his curiosity in pursuing the adventures of a person in whose favor he is prepossessed; he espouses his cause, he sympathizes with him in distress; his indignation is heated against the authors of his calamity; the humane passions are inflamed; the contrast between dejected virtue and insulting vice appears with greater aggravation; and every impression having a double force on the imagination, the memory retains the circumstance, and the heart improves by the example. The attention is not tired with a bare catalogue of characters, but agreeably diverted with all the variety of invention; and the vicissitudes of life appear in their peculiar circumstances, opening an ample field for wit and humor.

Romance, no doubt, owes its origin to ignorance, vanity, and superstition. In the dark ages of the world, when a man had rendered himself

famous for wisdom or valor, his family and adherents availed themselves of his superior qualities, magnified his virtues, and represented his
character and person as sacred and supernatural.
The vulgar easily swallowed the bait, implored
his protection, and yielded the tribute of homage
and praise even to adoration; his exploits were
handed down to posterity with a thousand exaggerations; they were repeated as incitements to
virtue; divine honors were paid, and altars
erected to his memory, for the encouragement of
those who attempted to imitate his example; and
hence arose the heathen mythology, which is no
other than a collection of extravagant romances.
As learning advanced, and genius received cultivation, these stories were embellished with the
graces of poetry; that they might the better recommend themselves to the attention, they were
sung in public, at festivals, for the instruction
and delight of the audience; and rehearsed before
battle, as incentives to deeds of glory. Thus
tragedy and the epic muse were born, and, in the
progress of taste, arrived at perfection. It is no
wonder that the ancients could not relish a fable
in prose, after they had seen so many remarkable
events celebrated in verse, by their best poets;
we, therefore, find no romance among them, during the era of their excellence, unless the *Cyro-
pædia* of Xenophon may be so called; and it was
not till arts and sciences began to revive, after
the irruption of the Barbarians into Europe, that
anything of this kind appeared. But when the
minds of men were debauched, by the imposi-

tion of priestcraft, to the most absurd pitch of credulity, the authors of romance arose, and, losing sight of probability, filled their performances with the most monstrous hyperboles. If they could not equal the ancient poets in point of genius, they were resolved to excel them in fiction, and apply to the wonder rather than the judgment of their readers. Accordingly they brought necromancy to their aid, and instead of supporting the character of their heroes by dignity of sentiment and practice, distinguished them by their bodily strength, activity, and extravagance of behavior. Although nothing could be more ludicrous and unnatural than the figures they drew, they did not want patrons and admirers, and the world actually began to be infected with the spirit of knight-errantry, when Cervantes, by an inimitable piece of ridicule, reformed the taste of mankind, representing chivalry in the right point of view, and converting romance to purposes far more useful and entertaining, by making it assume the sock, and point out the follies of ordinary life.

The same method has been practiced by other Spanish and French authors, and by none more successfully than by Monsieur Le Sage, who, in his *Adventures of Gil Blas,* has described the knavery and foibles of life, with infinite humor and sagacity. The following sheets I have modeled on his plan, taking the liberty, however, to differ from him in the execution, where I thought his particular situations were uncommon, extravagant, or peculiar to the country in which the scene is laid. The disgraces of Gil Blas are, for the most part, such as rather excite mirth than compassion: he himself laughs at them; and his transitions from distress to happiness, or at least ease, are so sudden, that neither the reader has time to pity him, nor himself to be acquainted with affliction. This conduct, in my opinion, not only deviates from probability, but prevents that generous indignation which ought to animate the reader against the sordid and vicious disposition of the world.

I have attempted to represent modest merit struggling with every difficulty to which a friendless orphan is exposed, from his own want of experience, as well as from the selfishness, envy, malice, and base indifference of mankind. To secure a favorable prepossession, I have allowed him the advantages of birth and education, which, in the series of his misfortunes, will, I hope, engage the ingenuous more warmly in his behalf; and though I foresee that some people will be offended at the mean scenes in which he is involved, I persuade myself the judicious will not only perceive the necessity of describing those situations to which he must of course be confined, in his low state, but also find entertainment in viewing those parts of life, where the humors and passions are undisguised by affectation, ceremony, or education; and the whimsical peculiarities of disposition appear as nature has implanted them. But I believe I need not trouble myself in vindicating a practice authorized by the best writers in this way, some of whom I have already named.

Every intelligent reader will, at first sight, perceive I have not deviated from nature in the facts, which are all true in the main, although the circumstances are altered and disguised, to avoid personal satire.

It now remains to give my reasons for making the chief personage of this work a North Briton; which are chiefly these: I could at a small expense bestow on him such education as I thought the dignity of his birth and character required, which could not possibly be obtained in England, by such slender means as the nature of my plan would afford. In the next place, I could represent simplicity of manners in a remote part of the kingdom, with more propriety than in any other place near the capital; and, lastly, the disposition of the Scots, addicted to traveling, justifies my conduct in deriving an adventurer from that country.

That the delicate reader may not be offended at the unmeaning oaths which proceed from the mouths of some persons in these memoirs, I beg leave to premise, that I imagined nothing could more effectually expose the absurdity of such miserable expletives, than a natural and verbal representation of the discourse in which they occur.

APOLOGUE

A YOUNG painter, indulging a vein of pleasantry sketched a kind of conversation-
piece, representing a bear, an owl, a
monkey, and an ass; and to render it more strik-
ing, humorous, and moral, distinguished every
figure by some emblem of human life.

Bruin was exhibited in the garb and attitude
of an old, toothless, drunken soldier; the owl,
perched upon the handle of a coffee-pot, with
spectacles on his nose, seemed to contemplate a
newspaper; and the ass, ornamented with a huge
tye-wig (which, however, could not conceal his
long ears), sat for his picture to the monkey, who
appeared with the implements of painting. This
whimsical group afforded some mirth, and met
with general approbation, until some mischievous
wag hinted that the whole was a lampoon upon
the friends of the performer; an insinuation
which was no sooner circulated, than those very
people who applauded it before began to be
alarmed, and even to fancy themselves signified
by the several figures of the piece.

Among others, a worthy personage in years,
who had served in the army with reputation, being incensed at the supposed outrage, repaired to
the lodgings of the painter, and, finding him at
home, "Hark ye, Mr. Monkey," said he, "I have
a good mind to convince you, that though the

bear has lost his teeth, he retains his paws, and that he is not so drunk but he can perceive your impertinence—'Sblood! sir, that toothless jaw is a d—ned scandalous libel!—but don't you imagine me so chopfallen as not to be able to chew the cud of resentment.'' Here he was interrupted by the arrival of a learned physician, who, advancing to the culprit with fury in his aspect, exclaimed, ''Suppose the augmentation of the ass's ears should prove the diminution of the baboon's—nay, seek not to prevaricate, for by the beard of Esculapius! there is not one hair in this periwig that will not stand up in judgment to convict thee of personal abuse.—Do but observe, captain, how this pitiful little fellow has copied the very curls—the color, indeed, is different, but then the form and foretop are quite similar.'' While he thus remonstrated in a strain of vociferation, a venerable senator entered, and waddling up to the delinquent, ''Jackanapes!'' cried he, ''I will now let thee see I can read something else than a newspaper, and that, without the help of spectacles—here is your own note of hand, sirrah, for money which, if I had not advanced, you yourself would have resembled an owl, in not daring to show your face by day, you ungrateful slanderous knave!''

In vain the astonished painter declared that he had no intention to give offense, or to characterize particular persons: they affirmed the resemblance was too palpable to be overlooked; they taxed him with insolence, malice, and ingratitude; and their clamors being overheard by the public, the captain was a bear, the doctor an ass, and the senator an owl, to his dying day.

Christian reader, I beseech thee, in the bowels of the Lord, remember this example while thou art employed in the perusal of the following sheets; and seek not to appropriate to thyself that which equally belongs to five hundred different people. If thou shouldst meet with a character that reflects thee in some ungracious particular, keep thy own counsel; consider that one feature makes not a face, and that, though thou art, perhaps, distinguished by a bottle nose, twenty of thy neighbors may be in the same predicament.

THE ADVENTURES

OF

RODERICK RANDOM

CHAPTER ONE

Of my Birth and Parentage

I WAS born in the northern part of this united kingdom, in the house of my grandfather; a gentleman of considerable fortune and influence, who had, on many occasions, signalized himself in behalf of his country; and was remarkable for his abilities in the law, which he exercised with great success, in the station of a judge, particularly against beggars, for whom he had a singular aversion.

My father, his youngest son, falling in love with a poor relation, who lived with the old gentleman in quality of housekeeper, espoused her privately; and I was the first fruit of that marriage. During her pregnancy, a dream discomposed my mother so much, that her husband, tired with her importunity, at last consulted a Highland seer, whose favorable interpretation he would have secured beforehand by a bribe, but found him incorruptible. She dreamed she was delivered of a tennis-ball, which the devil (who, to her great surprise, acted the part of midwife) struck so forcibly with a racket, that it disappeared in an instant; and she was for some time inconsolable for the loss of her offspring; when all of a sudden, she beheld it return with equal violence, and enter the earth beneath her feet, whence immediately sprung up a goodly tree covered with blossoms, the scent of which operated so strongly on her nerves, that she awoke. The attentive sage, after some deliberation, assured my parents, that their firstborn would be a great traveler; that he would undergo many dangers and difficulties, and at last return to his native land, where he would flourish in happiness and reputation. How truly this was foretold, will appear in the sequel.

It was not long before some officious person informed my grandfather of certain familiarities that passed between his son and housekeeper, which alarmed him so much, that a few days after, he told my father it was high time for him to think of settling; and that he had provided a match for him, to which he could in justice have no objections. My father, finding it would be impossible to conceal his situation much longer, frankly owned what he had done, and excused himself for not having asked the consent of his father, by saying, he knew it would have been to no purpose; and that, had his inclination been known, my grandfather might have taken such measures as would have effectually put the gratification of it out of his power. He added, that no exceptions could be taken to his wife's virtue, birth, beauty, and good sense; and as for fortune, it was beneath his care. The old gentleman, who kept all his passions, except one, in excellent order, heard him to an end with great temper; and then calmly asked, how he proposed to maintain himself and spouse? He replied, he could be in no danger of wanting, while his father's tenderness remained, which he and his wife should always cultivate with the utmost veneration; that he was persuaded his allowance would be suitable to the dignity and circumstances of his family, and to the provision already made for his brothers and sisters, who were happily settled under his protection. "Your brothers and sisters," said my grandfather, "did not think it beneath them to consult me in an affair of such importance as matrimony; neither, I suppose, would you have omitted that piece of duty, had not you some secret fund in reserve, to the comforts of which I leave you, with a desire that you will this night seek out another habitation for yourself and wife, whither, in a short time, I will send you an account of the expense I have been at in your education, with a view of being reimbursed. Sir, you have made the grand tour;—you are a polite gentleman,—a very pretty gentleman;—I wish you a great deal of joy, and am your very humble servant." So saying, he left my father in a situation easily imagined.

However, he did not long hesitate; for, being perfectly well acquainted with his father's disposition, he did not doubt that he was glad of this pretense to get rid of him; and his resolves being invariable as the laws of the Medes and

Persians, he knew it would be to no purpose to attempt him by prayers and entreaties; so, without any further application, he betook himself, with his disconsolate bedfellow, to a farmhouse, where an old servant of his mother dwelt. There they remained for some time in a situation but ill adapted to the elegance of their desires, and tenderness of their love; which, nevertheless, my father chose to endure, rather than supplicate an unnatural and inflexible parent. But my mother, foreseeing the inconvenience to which she must have been exposed, had she been delivered in this place (and her pregnancy was very far advanced), without communicating her design to her husband, went in disguise to the house of my grandfather, hoping that her tears and condition would move him to compassion, and reconcile him to an event which was now irrevocably past. She found means to deceive the servants, and was introduced as an unfortunate lady, who wanted to complain of some matrimonial grievances; it being my grandfather's particular province to decide in all cases of scandal. She was accordingly admitted into his presence; where discovering herself, she fell at his feet, and in the most affecting manner implored his forgiveness; at the same time representing the danger that threatened not only her life, but that of his own grandchild, which was about to see the light.

He told her, he was sorry that the indiscretion of her and his son had compelled him to make a vow, which put it out of his power to give them any assistance; that he had already imparted his thoughts on that subject to her husband, and was surprised that they should disturb his peace with any further importunity. This said, he retired. The violence of my mother's affliction had such an effect on her constitution, that she was immediately seized with the pains of childbed; and had not an old maid-servant, to whom she was very dear, afforded her pity and assistance, at the hazard of incurring my grandfather's displeasure, she and the innocent fruit of her womb must have fallen miserable victims to his rigor and inhumanity. By the friendship of this poor woman, she was carried up to a garret, and immediately delivered of a man-child, the story of whose unfortunate birth he himself now relates. My father being informed of what had happened, flew to the embraces of his darling spouse, and, while he loaded his offspring with paternal caresses, could not forbear shedding a flood of tears, on beholding the dear partner of his heart, for whose ease he would have sacrificed the treasures of the East, stretched upon a flock bed in a miserable apartment, unable to protect her from the inclemencies of the weather. It is not to be supposed, that the old gentleman was ignorant of what passed, though he affected to know nothing of the matter, and pretended to be very much surprised, when one of his grandchildren, by his eldest son deceased, who lived with him as his heir-apparent, acquainted him with the affair. He determined, therefore, to observe no medium, but immediately, on the third day after her delivery, sent her a peremptory order to be gone, and turned off the servant who had preserved her life.

This behavior so exasperated my father, that he had recourse to the most dreadful imprecations; and, on his bare knees, implored that heaven would renounce him, if ever he should forget or forgive the barbarity of his sire. The injuries which this unhappy mother received from her removal in such circumstances, and the want of necessaries where she lodged, together with her grief and anxiety of mind, soon threw her into a languishing disorder, which put an end to her life. My father, who loved her tenderly, was so affected with her death, that he remained six weeks deprived of his senses; during which time, the people where he lodged carried the infant to the old man, who relented so far, on hearing the melancholy story of his daughter-in-law's death, and the deplorable condition of his son, as to send the child to nurse; and he ordered my father to be carried home to his house, where he soon recovered the use of his reason. Whether this hardhearted judge felt any remorse for his cruel treatment of his son and daughter, or (which is more probable) was afraid his character would suffer in the neighborhood, he professed great sorrow for his conduct to my father, whose delirium was succeeded by a profound melancholy and reserve. At length he disappeared, and, notwithstanding all imaginable inquiry, could not be heard of; a circumstance which confirmed most people in the opinion of his having made away with himself in a fit of despair. How I understood the particulars of my birth, will appear in the course of these memoirs.

CHAPTER TWO

THERE were not wanting some who suspected my uncles of being concerned in
my father's fate, on the supposition that
they would all share in the patrimony destined
for him; and this conjecture was strengthened by
reflecting, that, in all his calamities, they never
discovered the least inclination to serve him; but,
on the contrary, by all the artifices in their power,
fed his father's resentment, and supported his
resolution of leaving him to misery and want.
But people of judgment treated this situation as
an idle chimera; because, had my relations been
so wicked as to consult their interests by commit-
ting such an atrocious crime, the fate of my
father would have extended to me, too, whose life
was another obstacle to their expectation. Meanwhile, I grew apace; and as I strongly resembled
my father, who was the darling of the tenants, I
wanted nothing which their indigent circumstances could afford: but their favor was a weak
resource against the jealous enmity of my cousins; who, the more my infancy promised, con-

7

ceived the more implacable hatred against me;
and, before I was six years of age, had so effectually blockaded my grandfather, that I never
saw him but by stealth; when I sometimes made
up to his chair, as he sat to view his laborers in
the field: on which occasions, he would stroke my
head, bid me be a good boy, and promise to take
care of me. I was soon after sent to school at a
village hard by, of which he had been dictator
time out of mind; but as he neither paid for my
board, nor supplied me with clothes, books, and
other necessaries I required, my condition was
very ragged and contemptible; and the schoolmaster, who, through fear of my grandfather,
taught me *gratis*, gave himself no concern about
the progress I made under his instruction.

In spite of all these difficulties and disgraces,
I became a good proficient in the Latin tongue;
and as soon as I could write tolerably, pestered
my grandfather with letters to such a degree, that
he sent for my master, and chid him severely for
bestowing such pains on my education, telling
him, that if ever I should be brought to the gallows for forgery, which he had taught me to commit, my blood would lie on his head. The pedant,
who dreaded nothing more than the displeasure
of his patron, assured his honor, that the boy's
ability was more owing to his own genius and application, than to any instruction or encouragement he received; that, although he could not di-
vest him of the knowledge he had already imbibed, unless he would empower him to disable
his fingers, he should endeavor, with God's help,

to prevent his future improvement. And, indeed, he punctually performed what he had undertaken; for, on pretense that I had writ impertinent letters to my grandfather, he caused a board to be made with five holes in it, through which he thrust the fingers and thumb of my right hand, and fastened it with whipcord to my wrist, in such a manner as effectually debarred me the use of my pen. But this restraint I was freed from in a few days, by an accident which happened in a quarrel between me and another boy, who, taking upon him to insult my poverty, I was so incensed at his ungenerous reproach, that, with one stroke of my machine, I cut him to the skull, to the great terror of myself and schoolfellows, who left him bleeding on the ground, and ran to inform the master of what had happened. I was so severely punished for this trespass, that, were I to live to the age of Methusalem, the impression it made on me would not be effaced; no more than the antipathy and horror I conceived for the merciless tyrant who inflicted it. The contempt which my appearance naturally produced in all who saw me, the continual wants to which I was exposed, and my own haughty disposition, impatient of affronts, involved me in a thousand troublesome adventures, by which I was at length inured to adversity, and emboldened to undertakings far above my years. I was often inhumanly scourged for crimes I did not commit; because, having the character of a vagabond in the village every piece of mischief, whose author lay unknown, was charged upon me. I have been found

guilty of robbing orchards I never entered, of
killing cats I never hurted, of stealing gingerbread I never touched, and of abusing old women
I never saw. Nay, a stammering carpenter had
eloquence enough to persuade my master that I
fired a pistol, loaded with small shot, into his
window; though my landlady and the whole family bore witness, that I was a-bed fast asleep at
the time when this outrage was committed. I was
once flogged for having narrowly escaped drown-
ing, by the sinking of a ferry-boat in which I was
passenger; another time for having recovered of
a bruise occasioned by a horse and cart running
over me; a third time for being bit by a baker's
dog. In short, whether I was guilty or unfortunate, the correction and sympathy of this arbitrary pedagogue were the same.

Far from being subdued by this infernal usage,
my indignation triumphed over that slavish awe
which had hitherto enforced my obedience; and
the more my years and knowledge increased, the
more I perceived the injustice and barbarity of
his behavior. By the help of an uncommon genius, and the advice and direction of our usher,
who had served my father in his travels, I made
a surprising progress in the classics, writing, and
arithmetic; so that, before I was twelve years old,
I was allowed by everybody to be the best scholar
in the school. This qualification, together with
a boldness of temper, and strength of make, which
had subjected almost all my contemporaries, gave
me such influence over them, that I began to form
cabals against my persecutor, and was in hopes

of being able to bid him defiance in a very short
time. Being at the head of a faction consisting
of thirty boys, most of them of my own age, I was
determined to put their metal to trial, that I might
know how far they were to be depended upon,
before I put my grand scheme in execution: with
this view, we attacked a body of stout apprentices,
who had taken possession of a part of the ground
allotted to us for the scene of our diversions, and
who were then playing at nine-pins on the spot:
but I had the mortification to see my adherents
routed in an instant, and a leg of one of them
broke in his flight, by the bowl, which one of our
adversaries had detached in pursuit of us. This
discomfiture did not hinder us from engaging
them afterward in frequent skirmishes, which we
maintained by throwing stones at a distance,
wherein I received many wounds, the scars of
which still remain. Our enemies were so har-
assed and interrupted by these alarms, that they
at last abandoned their conquest, and left us to
the peaceable enjoyment of our own territories.
It would be endless to enumerate the exploits we
performed in the course of this confederacy,
which became the terror of the whole village; in-
somuch, that when different interests divided it,
one of the parties commonly courted the assistance of Roderick Random (by which name I was
known), to cast the balance, and keep the opposite
faction in awe.

Meanwhile, I took the advantage of every play-
day to present myself before my grandfather, to
whom I seldom found access, by reason of his be-

ing closely besieged by a numerous family of his female grandchildren, who, though they perpetually quarreled among themselves, never failed to join against me, as the common enemy of all. His heir, who was about the age of eighteen, minded nothing but fox-hunting, and, indeed, was qualified for nothing else, notwithstanding his grandfather's indulgence, in entertaining a tutor for him at home, who at the same time performed the office of parish-clerk. This young Actæon, who inherited his grandfather's antipathy to everything in distress, never set eyes on me, without uncoupling his beagles, and hunting me into some cottage or other, whither I generally fled for snelter. In this Christian amusement, he was encouraged by his preceptor, who, no doubt, took such opportunities to ingratiate himself with the rising sun, observing that the old gentleman, according to the course of nature, had not long to live, for he was already on the verge of fourscore. The behavior of this rascally sycophant incensed me so much, that one day, when I was beleaguered by him and his hounds in a farmer's house, where I had found protection, I took aim at him (being an excellent marksman) with a large pebble, which struck out four of his fore-teeth, and effectually incapacitated him for doing the office of a clerk.

CHAPTER THREE

ABOUT this time, my mother's only brother, who had been long abroad, lieutenant of a man-of-war, arrived in his own country; where, being informed of my condition, he came to see me, and, out of his slender finances, not only supplied me with what necessaries I wanted for the present, but resolved not to leave the country until he had prevailed on my grandfather to settle something handsome on me for the future. This was a task to which he was by no means equal, being entirely ignorant, not only of the judge's disposition, but also unacquainted with the ways of men in general, to which his education on board had kept him an utter stranger. He was a strong built man, somewhat bandy-legged, with a neck like that of a bull, and a face which, you might easily perceive, had withstood the most obstinate assaults of the weather. His dress consisted of a soldier's coat, altered for him by the ship's tailor, a striped flannel jacket, a pair of red breeches, japanned with pitch, clean gray worsted stockings, large silver buckles, that cov-

13

ered three-fourths of his shoes, a silver-laced hat, whose crown overlooked the brims about an inch and a half, a black bob wig in buckle, a check shirt, a silk handkerchief, an hanger with a brass handle, girded to his thigh by a tarnished laced belt, and a good oak plant under his arm.

Thus equipped, he set out with me (who, by his bounty, made a very decent appearance,) for my grandfather's house, where we were saluted by Jowler and Cæsar, whom my cousin, young master, had let loose at our approach. Being well acquainted with the inveteracy of these curs, I was about to take myself to my heels, when my uncle seized me with one hand, brandished his cudgel with the other, and at one blow laid Cæsar sprawling on the ground; but finding himself attacked at the same time in the rear by Jowler, and fearing Cæsar might recover, he drew his hanger, wheeled about, and, by a lucky stroke, severed Jowler's head from his body. By this time the young fox-hunter and three servants, armed with pitchforks and flails, were come to the assistance of the dogs, whom they found breathless upon the field; and my cousin was so provoked at the death of his favorites, that he ordered his attendants to advance and take vengeance on their executioner, whom he loaded with all the curses and reproaches his anger could suggest. Upon which my uncle stepped forward with an undaunted air, at the sight of whose bloody weapon his antagonists fell back with precipitation, when he accosted their leader thus: "Lookee, brother, your dogs have boarded me without provocation; what I did was

in my own defense. So you had best be civil, and
let us shoot ahead clear of you." Whether the
young squire misinterpreted my uncle's desire of
peace, or was enraged at the fate of his hounds
beyond his usual pitch of resolution, I know not;
but he snatched a flail from one of his followers,
and came up with a show of assaulting the lieutenant, who, putting himself in a posture of defense, proceeded thus: "Lookee, you lubberly
son of a w—e, if you come athwart me, 'ware your
gingerbread work; I'll be foul of your quarter,
d—n me." This declaration, followed by a flourish of his hanger, seemed to check the progress
of the young gentleman's choler, who, looking behind him, perceived his attendants had slunk into
the house, shut the gate, and left him to decide
the contention by himself. Here a parley ensued,
which was introduced by my cousin's asking,
"Who the d—l are you? What do you want?—
Some scoundrel of a seaman, I suppose, who has
deserted, and turned thief. But don't think you
shall escape, sirrah; I'll have you hanged, you
dog, I will; your blood shall pay for that of my
two hounds, you ragamuffin. I would not have
parted with them to save your whole generation
from the gallows, you ruffian, you." "None of
your jaw, you swab—none of your jaw," replied
my uncle—"else I shall trim your laced jacket
for you—I shall rub you down with an oaken
towel, my boy—I shall."

So saying, he sheathed his hanger, and grasped
his cudgel. Meanwhile, the people of the house
being alarmed, one of my female cousins opened

a window, and asked what was the matter? "The
matter!" answered the lieutenant, "no great matter, young woman. I have business with the old
gentleman, and this spark, belike, won't allow me
to come alongside of him, that's all." After a
few minutes' pause, we were admitted, and conducted to my grandfather's chamber, through a
lane of my relations, who honored me with very
significant looks, as I passed along. When we
came into the judge's presence, my uncle, after
two or three sea-bows, expressed himself in this
manner: "Your servant—your servant. What
cheer, father?—what cheer?—I suppose you don't
know me—mayhap you don't. My name is Tom
Bowling; and this here boy—you look as if you
did not know him neither; 'tis like you mayn't.
He's new rigg'd, i'faith; his cloth don't shake in
the wind so much as it wont to do. 'Tis my
nephew, d'ye see, Roderick Random—your own
flesh and blood, old gentleman. Don't lag astern,
you dog" (pulling me forward). My grandfather, who was laid up with the gout, received
this relation, after his long absence, with that
coldness of civility which was peculiar to him;
told him he was glad to see him, and desired him
to sit down. "Thank ye, thank ye, sir, I had as
lief stand," said my uncle. "For my own part, I
desire nothing of you; but if you have any conscience at all, do something for this poor boy, who
has been used at a very unchristian rate. Unchristian, do I call it? I am sure the Moors in
Barbary have more humanity than to leave their
little ones to want. I would fain know why my

sister's son is more neglected than that there fair-
weather Jack," (pointing to the young squire,
who, with the rest of my cousins, had followed us
into the room). "Is not he as near akin to you as
the other? Is not he much handsomer and better
built than that great chucklehead? Come, come
—consider, old gentleman, you are going in a
short time to give an account of your evil actions.
Remember the wrongs you did his father; and
make all the satisfaction in your power, before it
be too late. The least thing you can do is to settle his father's portion on him."

The young ladies, who thought themselves too
much concerned to contain themselves any longer,
set up their throats all together against my pro-
tector: "Scurvy companion—saucy tarpaulin—
rude, impertinent fellow—did he think to pre-
scribe to grandpapa? His sister's brat had been
too well taken care of; grandpapa was too just
not to make a difference between an unnatural re-
bellious son, and his dutiful loving children, who
took his advice in all things"—and such expressions, were vented against him with great violence, until the judge at length commanded silence. He calmly rebuked my uncle for his un-
mannerly behavior, which he said he would excuse, on account of his education. He told him
he had been very kind to the boy, whom he had
kept to school seven or eight years, although he
was informed he made no progress in his learning, but was addicted to all manner of vice; which
he rather believed, because he himself was witness
to a barbarous piece of mischief he had committed

on the jaws of his chaplain. But, however, he would see what the lad was fit for, and bind him apprentice to some honest tradesman or other, provided he would mend his manners, and behave for the future as became him.

The honest tar, whose pride and indignation boiled within him, answered my grandfather, that it was true he had sent him to school, but it had cost him nothing; for he had never been at one shilling expense to furnish him with food, raiment, books, or other necessaries; so that it was not to be much wondered at, if the boy made small progress; and yet, whoever told him so, was a lying lubberly rascal, and deserved to be keel-hauled. For though he (the lieutenant) did not understand those matters himself, he was well informed as how Rory was the best scholar of his age in all the country; the truth of which he would maintain, by laying a wager of his whole half-year's pay on the boy's head; (with these words, he pulled out his purse, and challenged the company). "Neither is he predicted to vice, as you affirm, but rather left like a wreck, d'ye see, at the mercy of the wind and weather by your neglect, old gentleman. As for what happened to your chaplain, I am only sorry that he did not knock out the scoundrel's brains, instead of his teeth. By the Lord, if ever I come up with him, he had better be in Greenland—that's all. Thank you for your courteous offer of binding the lad apprentice to a tradesman. I suppose you would make a tailor of him—would you? I had rather see him hanged, d'ye see. Come along, Rory, I perceive how the land lies, my boy; let's tack about—i'faith, while I have a shilling, thou shan't want a tester. B'wye, old gentleman, you're bound for the other world, but I believe damnably ill provided for the voyage." Thus ended our visit, and we returned to the village, my uncle muttering curses all the way against the old shark and the young fry that surrounded him.

CHAPTER FOUR

My Grandfather makes his Will—Our second Visit—He dies—
His Will is read in presence of all his living Descendants
—The Disappointment of my female Cousins—My Uncle's
Behavior.

A FEW weeks after our first visit, we were
informed that the old judge, at the end
of a fit of thoughtfulness which lasted
three days, had sent for a notary, and made his
will; that the distemper had mounted from his
legs to his stomach, and, being conscious of his
approaching end, he had desired to see all his
descendants without exception. In obedience to
this summons, my uncle set out with me a second
time, to receive the last benediction of my grandfather: often repeating by the road, "Ey, ey, we
have brought up the old hulk at last. You shall
see—you shall see the effect of my admonition."
When we entered his chamber, which was crowded
with his relations, we advanced to the bedside,
where we found him in his last agonies, supported
by two of his granddaughters, who sat on each
side of him, sobbing most piteously, and wiping
away the froth and slaver as it gathered on his
lips, which they frequently kissed with a show of
great anguish and affection. My uncle approached him with these words: "What! he's
not aweigh? How fare ye, old gentleman?—Lord

20

have mercy upon your poor sinful soul." Upon which the dying man turned his languid eyes toward us, and Mr. Bowling went on, "Here's poor Rory come to see you before you die, and receive your blessing. What, man! don't despair—you have been a great sinner, 'tis true, what then? There's a righteous judge above—a'nt there?— He minds me no more than a porpoise. Yes, yes, he's agoing—the land crabs will have him, I see that—his anchor's apeak, i'faith."

This homely consolation scandalized the company so much, and especially the parson, who probably thought his province invaded, that we were obliged to retire into the other room, where, in a few minutes, we were convinced of my grandfather's decease, by a dismal yell uttered by the young ladies in his apartment; whither we immediately hastened, and found his heir, who had retired a little before into a closet, under pretense of giving vent to his sorrow, asking, with a countenance beslubbered with tears, if his grandpapa was certainly dead?—"Dead!" says my uncle, looking at the body, "ay, ay, I'll warrant him as dead as a herring. Odds fish! now my dream is out for all the world. I thought I stood upon the forecastle, and saw a parcel of carrion crows foul of a dead shark that floated alongside, and the devil perching on our sprit-sail yard, in the likeness of a blue bear—who, d'ye see, jumped overboard upon the carcass, and carried it to the bottom in his claws." "Out upon thee, reprobate!" cries the parson, "out upon thee, blasphemous wretch!—Dost thou think his honor's soul is in the possession of Satan?'' The clamor immediately arose, and my poor uncle, being shouldered from one corner of the room to the other, was obliged to lug out in his own defense, and swear he would turn out for no man, till such time as he knew who had a title to send him adrift. ''None of your tricks upon travelers,'' said he; ''mayhap old bluff has left my kinsman here his heir: if he has, it will be the better for his miserable soul. Odds bob! I'd desire no better news. I'd soon make him a clear ship, I warrant you.'' To avoid any further disturbance, one of my grandfather's executors, who was present, assured Mr. Bowling that his nephew should have all manner of justice; that a day should be appointed, after the funeral, for examining the papers of the deceased, in presence of all his relations; till which time every desk and cabinet in the house should remain close sealed; and that he was very welcome to be witness to this ceremony, which was immediately performed to his satisfaction. In the meantime, orders were given to provide mourning for all the relations, in which number I was included: but my uncle would not suffer me to accept of it, until I should be assured whether or not I had reason to honor his memory so far.

During this interval, the conjectures of people, with regard to the old gentleman's will, were various. As it was well known he had, besides his landed estate, which was worth £700 per annum, six or seven thousand pounds at interest, some imagined, that the whole real estate (which he had greatly improved) would go to the young man whom he always entertained as his heir; and that the money would be equally divided between my female cousins (five in number) and me. Others were of opinion, that as the rest of his children had been already provided for, he would only bequeath two or three hundred pounds to each of his granddaughters, and leave the bulk of the sum to me, to atone for his unnatural usage of my father. At length the important hour arrived, and the will was produced in the midst of the expectants, whose looks and gestures formed a group that would have been very entertaining to an unconcerned spectator. But the reader can scarce conceive the astonishment and mortification that appeared, when the attorney pronounced aloud, the young squire sole heir of all his grandfather's estate, personal and real. My uncle, who had listened with great attention, sucking the head of his cudgel all the while, accompanied these words of the attorney with a stare, and *whew,* that alarmed the whole assembly. The eldest and pertest of my female competitors, who had been always very officious about my grandfather's person, inquired with a faltering accent, and visage as yellow as an orange, "If there were no legacies?" and was answered, "None at all." Upon which she fainted away. The rest, whose expectations, perhaps, were not so sanguine, supported their disappointment with more resolution; though not without giving evident marks of indignation, and grief at least as genuine as that which appeared in them at the old gentleman's death. My conductor, after having kicked with his heel for some time against the wainscot, began: "So there's no legacy, friend, ha!—here's an old succubus;—but somebody's soul howls for it, d—n me!" The parson of the parish, who was one of the executors, and had acted as ghostly director to the old man, no sooner heard this exclamation than he cried out, "Avaunt, unchristian reviler! avaunt!—wilt thou not allow the soul of his honor to rest in peace?" But this zealous pastor did not find himself so warmly seconded, as formerly, by the young ladies, who now joined my uncle against him, and accused him of having acted the part of a busy-body with their grandpapa, whose ears he had certainly abused by false stories to their prejudice, or else he would not have neglected them in such an unnatural manner. The young squire was much diverted with this scene, and whispered to my uncle, that, if he had not murdered his dogs, he would have shown him glorious fun, by hunting a black badger (so he termed the clergyman). The surly lieutenant, who was not in an humor to relish this amusement, replied, "You and your dogs may be d—d; I suppose you'll find them with your old dad, in the latitude of hell. Come, Rory—about ship, my lad—we must steer another course, I think."— And away we went.

CHAPTER FIVE

O N our way back to the village, my uncle
spoke not a word during the space of a
whole hour, but whistled, with great vehemence, the tune of "Why should we quarrel for
riches," etc., his visage being contracted all the
while into a most formidable frown. At length
his pace increased to such a degree, that I was
left behind a considerable way. Then he waited
for me; and, when I was almost up with him,
called out in a surly tone, "Bear a hand, damme!
must I bring-to every minute for you, you lazy
dog?" Then, laying hold of me by the arm,
hauled me along, until his good nature, of which
he had a great share, and reflection getting the
better of his passion, he said, "Come, my boy,
don't be cast down—the old rascal is in hell—
that's some satisfaction; you shall go to sea with
me, my lad.—'A light heart and a thin pair of
breeches goes through the world, brave boys,'
as the song goes, eh!" Though this proposal did
not at all suit my inclination, I was afraid of discovering any aversion to it, lest I should disoblige the only friend I had in the world; and he

was so much a seaman, that he never dreamed I
could have any objection to his design, consequently gave himself no trouble in consulting my
approbation. But this resolution was soon
dropt, by the advice of our usher, who assured
Mr. Bowling, it would be a thousand pities to
balk my genius, which would certainly, one day,
make my fortune on shore, provided it received
due cultivation. Upon which this generous tar
determined, though he could ill afford it, to give
me university education; and accordingly settled
my board and other expenses, at a town not many
miles distant, famous for its colleges, whither we
repaired in a short time. But, before the day of
our departure, the schoolmaster, who no longer
had the fear of my grandfather before his eyes,
laid aside all decency and restraint, and not only
abused me in the grossest language his rancor
could suggest, as a wicked, profligate, dull, beg-
garly miscreant, whom he had taught out of charity; but also inveighed in the most bitter manner
against the memory of the judge (who, by the by,
had procured that settlement for him), hinting
in pretty plain terms, that the old gentleman's
soul was damn'd to all eternity, for his injustice
in neglecting to pay for my learning.

This brutal behavior, added to the sufferings I
had formerly undergone, made me think it high
time to be revenged of this insolent pedagogue.
Having consulted my adherents, I found them all
staunch in their promises to stand by me; and our
scheme was this: in the afternoon preceding the
day of my departure for the university, I re-

solved to take the advantage of the usher's going
out to make water, which he regularly did at four
o'clock, and shut the great door, that he might
not come to the assistance of his superior. This
being done, the assault was to be begun, by my
advancing to my master, and spitting in his face.
I was to be seconded by two of the strongest boys
in the school, who were devoted to me; their
business was to join me in dragging the tyrant to
a bench, over which he was to be laid, and his
bare posteriors heartily flogged with his own
birch, which we proposed to wrest from him in
the struggle; but if we should find him too many
for us all three, we were to demand the assistance
of our competitors, who should be ready to re-
inforce us, or oppose anything that might be undertaken for the master's relief. One of my principal assistants was called Jeremy Gawky, son
and heir of a wealthy gentleman in the neighborhood; and the name of the other, Hugh Strap, the
cadet of a family which had given shoemakers to
the village time out of mind. I had once saved
Gawky's life, by plunging into a river, and dragging him on shore, when he was on the point of
being drowned. I had often rescued him from
the clutches of those whom his insufferable ar-
rogance had provoked to a resentment he was not
able to sustain; and many times saved his reputation and posteriors, by performing his exercises
at school; so that it is not to be wondered at if
he had a particular regard for me and my interests. The attachment of Strap flowed from a
voluntary disinterested inclination, which had

manifested itself on many occasions on my behalf,
he having once rendered me the same service that
I had done Gawky, by saving my life at the risk
of his own; and often fathered offenses that I had
committed, for which he suffered severely, rather
than I should feel the weight of the punishment
I deserved. These two champions were the more
willing to engage in this enterprise, because they
intended to leave the school the next day as well as
I, the first being ordered by his father to return
into the country, and the other being bound apprentice to a barber, at a market town not far off.

In the meantime, my uncle being informed of
my master's behavior to me, was enraged at his
insolence, and vowed revenge so heartily, that I
could not refrain from telling him the scheme I
had concerted, which he heard with great satisfaction, at every sentence squirting out a mouthful
of spittle, tinctured with tobacco, of which he
constantly chewed a large quid. At last, pulling
up his breeches, he cried, "No, no, z—ds! that
won't do, neither. Howsomever, 'tis a bold undertaking, my lad, that I must say, i'faith! But,
lookee, lookee, how dost propose to get clear
off?—won't the enemy give chase, my boy? ay,
ay, that he will, I warrant, and alarm thè whole
coast. Ah! God help thee, more said than bal-
last, Rory. Let me alone for that—leave the
whole to me—I'll show him the foretop-sail, I
will. If so be your shipmates are jolly boys, and
won't flinch, you shall see, you shall see; egad,
I'll play him a salt-water trick; I'll bring him to
the gangway, and anoint him with a cat-o'-nine-

tails; he shall have a round dozen doubled, my lad, he shall, and be left lashed to his meditations.''

We were very proud of our associate, who immediately went to work, and prepared the instrument of his revenge with great skill and expedition; after which, he ordered our baggage to be packed up, and sent off a day before our attempt, and got horses ready to be mounted, as soon as the affair should be over. At length the hour arrived, when our auxiliary, seizing the opportunity of the usher's absence, bolted in, secured the door, and immediately laid hold of the pedant by his collar, who bawled out, ''Murder! thieves!'' with the voice of a Stentor. Though I trembled all over like an aspen-leaf, I knew there was no time to be lost, and accordingly got up, and summoned our associates to my assistance. Strap, without any hesitation, obeyed the signal; and seeing me leap upon the master's back, ran immediately to one of his legs, which, pulling with all his force, his dreadful adversary was humbled to the ground; upon which Gawky, who had hitherto remained in his place, under the influence of an universal trepidation, hastened to the scene of action, and insulted the fallen tyrant with a loud huzza, in which the whole school joined.

This noise alarmed the usher, who, finding himself shut out, endeavored, partly by threats, and partly by entreaties, to procure admission. My uncle bade him have a little patience, and he would let him in presently; but, if he pretended to move from that place, it should fare worse with the son of a b—h, his superior, on whom he intended only to bestow a little wholesome chastisement, for his barbarous usage of Rory; "to which," said he, "you are no stranger." By this time we had dragged the criminal to a post, to which Bowling tied him with a rope he had provided on purpose, after having secured his hands, and stripped his back. In this ludicrous posture he stood (to the no small entertainment of the boys, who crowded about him, and shouted with great exultation at the novelty of the sight), venting bitter imprecations against the lieutenant, and reproaching his scholars with treachery and rebellion, when the usher was admitted, whom my uncle accosted in this manner: "Harkee, Mr. Syntax, I believe you are an honest man, d'ye see, and I have a respect for you; but, for all that, we must, for our own security, d'ye see, belay you for a short time." With these words, he pulled out some fathoms of cord, which the honest man no sooner saw, than he protested with great earnestness he would allow no violence to be offered to him; at the same time accusing me of perfidy and ingratitude. But Bowling representing that it was in vain to resist, and that he did not mean to use him with violence and indecency, but only to hinder him from raising the hue and cry against us before we should be out of their power, he allowed himself to be bound to his own desk, where he sat a spectator of the punishment inflicted on his principal. My uncle having upbraided this arbitrary wretch with his inhumanity to me, told him that he proposed to give him a little discipline for the good of his soul, which he immediately put in practice with great vigor and dexterity. This smart application to the pedant's withered posteriors, gave him such exquisite pain, that he roared like a mad bull, danced, cursed, and blasphemed, like a frantic bedlamite. When the lieutenant thought himself sufficiently revenged, he took his leave of him in these words: "Now, friend, you'll remember me the longest day you have to live; I have given you a lesson that will let you know what flogging is, and teach you to have more sympathy for the future—shout, boys, shout." This ceremony was no sooner over, than my uncle proposed they should quit the school, and convoy their old comrade Rory to a public-house, about a mile from the village, where he would treat them all. His offer being joyfully embraced, he addressed himself to Mr. Syntax, and begged him to accompany us; but this invitation he refused with great disdain, telling my benefactor he was not the man he took him to be. "Well, well, old surly," replied my uncle, shaking his hand, "thou art an honest fellow notwithstanding; and if ever I have the command of a ship, thou shalt be our schoolmaster, i'faith." So saying, he dismissed the boys, and locking the door, left the two preceptors to console one another, while we moved forward on our journey, attended by a numerous retinue, whom he treated according to his promise. We parted with many tears, and lay that night at an inn on the road, about ten miles short of the town where I was to remain, at which we arrived the next day; and I found I had no cause to complain of the accommodations provided for me, in being boarded at the house of an apothecary, who had married a distant relation of my mother. In a few days after, my uncle set out for his ship, having settled the necessary funds for my maintenance and education.

CHAPTER SIX

I make great progress in my Studies—Am caressed by Everybody—My female Cousins take notice of me—I reject their Invitation—They are incensed and conspire against me—I am left destitute by a Misfortune that befalls my Uncle—Gawky's Treachery—My Revenge.

AS I was now capable of reflection, I began to consider my precarious situation; that I was utterly abandoned by those whose duty it was to protect me; and that my sole dependence was on the generosity of one man, who was not only exposed by his profession to continual dangers, which might one day deprive me of him forever; but also, no doubt, subject to those vicissitudes of disposition which a change of fortune usually creates, or which a better acquaintance with the world might produce; for I always ascribed his benevolence to the dictates of a heart as yet undebauched by a commerce with mankind. Alarmed at these considerations, I resolved to apply myself with great care to my studies, and enjoy the opportunity in my power: this I did with such success, that, in the space of three years, I understood Greek very well, was pretty far advanced in the mathematics, and no stranger to moral and natural philosophy; logic I made no account of; but, above all things, I valued myself on my taste in the *Belles Lettres,* and a talent for poetry, which had already produced some pieces that met with a very favorable reception. These qualifications, added to a good face and shape, acquired the esteem and acquaintance of the most considerable people in town; and I had the satisfaction to find myself in some degree of favor with the ladies—an intoxicating piece of good fortune to one of my amorous complexion!—which I obtained, or, at least, preserved, by gratifying their propensity to scandal in lampooning their rivals. Two of my female cousins lived in this place with their mother, since the death of their father, who left his whole fortune equally divided between them; so that, if they were not the most beautiful, they were at least the richest toasts in town, and received daily the addresses of all the beaux and cavaliers of the country. Although I had hitherto been looked upon by them with the most supercilious contempt, my character now attracted their notice so much, that I was given to understand I might be honored with their acquaintance, if I pleased.

The reader will easily perceive that this condescension either flowed from the hope of making my poetical capacity subservient to their malice, or, at least, of screening themselves from the lash of my resentment, which they had effectually provoked. I enjoyed this triumph with great satisfaction; and not only rejected their offer with disdain, but, in all my performances, whether satire or panegyric, industriously avoided mentioning their names, even while I celebrated those of their intimates. This neglect mortified their pride ex-

ceedingly, and incensed them to such a degree,
that they were resolved to make me repent of my
indifference. The first stroke of their revenge
consisted in their hiring a poor collegian to write
verses against me, the subject of which was my
own poverty, and the catastrophe of my unhappy
parents. But, besides the badness of the composition (of which they themselves were
ashamed), they did not find their account in en-
deavoring to reproach me with those misfortunes
which they and their relations had brought upon
me, and which, consequently, reflected much more
dishonor on themselves than on me, who was the
innocent victim of their barbarity and avarice.
Finding this plan miscarry, they found means to
irritate a young gentleman against me, by telling
him I had lampooned his mistress; and so effectually succeeded in the quality of incendiaries,
that this enraged lover determined to seize me
next night, as I returned to my lodgings from
a friend's house that I frequented. With this
view, he waited in the street, attended by two of
his companions, to whom he had imparted his
design, of carrying me down to the river, in which
he proposed to have me heartily ducked, notwithstanding the severity of the weather, it being then
about the middle of December. But this strata-
gem did not succeed; for, being apprised of their
ambush, I got home another way, and, by the
help of my landlord's apprentice, discharged a
volley from the garret window, which did great
execution upon them; and, next day, occasioned
so much mirth at their expense, that they found

themselves under a necessity of leaving the town,
until the adventure should be entirely forgotten.
My cousins, though twice baffled in their expectation, did not, however, desist from persecuting
me, who had now enraged them beyond a possibility of forgiveness, by detecting their malice,
and preventing its effects. Neither should I have
found them more humane, had I patiently sub-
mitted to their rancor, and bor[n]e, without mur-
muring, the rigor of their unreasonable hate; for
I have found, by experience, that, though small
favors may be acknowledged, and slight injuries
atoned, there is no wretch so ungrateful as he
whom you have most generously obliged, and no
enemy so implacable as those who have done you
the greatest wrong. These good-natured creatures, therefore, had recourse to a scheme which
conspired, with a piece of bad news I soon after
received, to give them all the satisfaction they desired.

This plan was to debauch the faith of my companion and confidant, who betrayed the trust I re-
posed in him, by imparting to them the particulars of my small amours, which they published
with such exaggerations, that I suffered very
much in the opinion of everybody, and was utterly discarded by the dear creatures whose names
had been called in question. While I was busy
in tracing out the author of this treachery, that I
might not only be revenged on him, but also vindicate my character to my friends, I one day perceived the looks of my landlady much altered when
I went home to dinner, and inquiring into the

cause, she screwed up her mouth, and fixing her
eyes on the ground, told me her husband had
received a letter from Mr. Bowling, with one en-
closed for me—she was very sorry for what had
happened, both for my sake and his own—people should be more cautious of their conduct. She
was always afraid his brutal behavior would bring
him into some misfortune or other. As for her
part, she would be very ready to befriend me, but
she had a small family of her own to maintain.
The world would do nothing for her if she should
come to want—charity begins at home. She
wished I had been bound to some substantial
handicraft, such as a weaver, or a shoemaker,
rather than loiter away my time in learning fool-
ish nonsense that would never bring me in a penny
—but some folks are wise, and some are otherwise. I was listening to this mysterious discourse
with great amazement, when her husband entered,
and, without speaking a syllable, put both the letters into my hand. I received them trembling,
and read what follows:—

To Mr. Roger Potion.

"Sir,—This is to let you know that I have quitted the
Thunder man of war, being obliged to sheer off, for killing
my captain, which I did fairly on the beach at Cape Tiberoon,
in the island of Hispaniola; having received his fire, and returned it, which went through his body. And I would serve
the best man so that ever stept between stem and stern, if so
be that he struck me, as Captain Oakum did. I am, thank
God, safe among the French, who are very civil, thof I don't
understand their lingo; and I hope to be restored in a little
time, for all the great friends and parliamentary interest of
the captain, for I have sent over to my landlord in Deal an

account of the whole affair, with our bearings and distances
while we were engaged, whereby I have desired him to lay it
before his Majesty, who (God bless him) will not suffer an
honest tar to be wronged. My love to your spouse, and
am

"Your loving friend and servant to command, while
"THOMAS BOWLING."

———

TO RODERICK RANDOM.

"DEAR RORY,—Don't be grieved at my misfortune; but
mind your book, my lad. I have got no money to send you;
but what of that?—Mr. Potion will take care of you, for
the love he bears me, and let you want for nothing, and it
shall go hard but I will see him one day repaid. No more
at present, but rests

"Your dutiful uncle and servant till death,
"THOMAS BOWLING."

This letter, which with the other was dated
from Port Louis in Hispaniola, I had no sooner
read, than the apothecary, shaking his head, began: "I have a very great regard for Mr. Bowling, that's certain,—and could be well content—
but times are very hard. There's no such thing
as money to be got—I believe 'tis all vanished
under ground, for my part. Besides, I have been
out of pocket already, having entertained you
since the beginning of this month without receiving a sixpence,—and God knows if ever I shall;
—for I believe it will go hard with your uncle.
And more than that, I was thinking of giving
you warning, for I want your apartment for a
new 'prentice, whom I expect from the country
every hour. So I desire you will this week provide yourself with another lodging."

The indignation which this harangue inspired, gave me spirits to support my reverse of fortune, and to tell him, I despised his mean selfish disposition so much, that I would starve rather than be beholden to him for one single meal. Upon which, out of my pocket-money, I paid him to the last farthing of what I owed, and assured him I would not sleep another night under his roof. This said, I sallied out in a transport of rage and sorrow, without knowing whither to fly for shelter, having not one friend in the world capable of relieving me, and only three shillings in my purse. After giving way for a few minutes to the dictates of my rage, I went and hired a small bedroom, at the rate of one shilling and sixpence per week, which I was obliged to pay per advance, before the landlord would receive me. Thither I removed my luggage; and next morning got up, with a view of craving the advice and assistance of a person who had on all occasions loaded me with caresses, and made frequent offers of friendship, while I was under no necessity of accepting them. He received me with his wonted affability, and insisted on my breakfasting with him—a favor which I did not think fit to refuse. But, when I communicated the occasion of my visit, he appeared so disconcerted, that I concluded him wonderfully affected with the misery of my condition, and looked upon him as a man of the most extensive sympathy and benevolence. He did not leave me long under this mistake; for, recovering himself from his confusion, he told me, he was grieved at my misfortune, and desired

to know what had passed between my landlord
Mr. Potion and me.   Whereupon I recounted the
conversation; and when I repeated the answer I
made to his ungenerous remonstrance with regard
to my leaving his house, this pretended friend
affected a stare, and exclaimed, "Is it possible
you could behave so ill to the man who had treated
you so kindly all along!"   My surprise at hearing
this was not at all affected, whatever his might
be; and I gave him to understand, with some
warmth, that I did not imagine he would so un-
reasonably espouse the cause of a scoundrel, who
ought to be expelled from every social community.
This heat of mine gave him all the advantage he
desired over me, and our discourse, after much
altercation, concluded in his desiring never to see
me again in that place; to which desire I yielded
my consent, assuring him, that had I been as well
acquainted with his principles formerly as I was
now, he never should have had an opportunity of
making that request;—and thus we parted.

On my return I met my comrade, Squire Gawky,
whom his father had sent, some time ago, to town,
for his improvement in writing, dancing, fencing,
and other modish qualifications.   As I had lived
with him, since his arrival, on the footing of our
old intimacy, I made no scruple of informing him
of the lowness of my circumstances, and asking
a small supply of money, to answer my present
expense; upon which he pulled out a handful of
halfpence, with a shilling or two among them, and
swore that was all he had to keep his pocket till
next quarter-day, he having lost the greatest part

of his allowance the night before at billiards.
Though this assertion might very well be true, I
was extremely mortified at his indifference; for
he neither expressed any sympathy for my mis-
hap, nor desire of alleviating my distress; and
accordingly I left him without uttering one word.
But, when I afterward understood that he was
the person who had formerly betrayed me to the
malice of my cousins, to whom likewise he had
carried the tidings of my forlorn situation, which
afforded them great matter of triumph and exultation, I determined with myself to call him to a
severe account; for which purpose I borrowed a
sword, and wrote a challenge, desiring him to
meet me at a certain time and place, that I might
have an opportunity of punishing his perfidy, at
the expense of his blood. He accepted the invitation; and I betook myself to the field, though
not without feeling considerable repugnance to
the combat, which frequently attacked me in cold
sweats by the way: but the desire of revenge, the
shame of retracting, and hope of conquest, conspired to repel these unmanly symptoms of fear;
and I appeared on the plain with a good grace.
There I waited an hour beyond the time appointed, and was not ill-pleased to find he had no
mind to meet me; because I should have an opportunity of exposing his cowardice, displaying
my own courage, and of beating him soundly
wheresoever I should find him, without any dread
of the consequence. Elevated with these suggestions, which entirely banished all thoughts of my
deplorable condition, I went directly to Gawky's

lodgings, where I was informed of his precipitate retreat, he having set out for the country in less than an hour after he had received my billet: and I was vain enough to have the whole story inserted in the news, although I was fain to sell a gold-laced hat to my landlord, for less than half price, to defray the expense, and contribute to my subsistence.

CHAPTER SEVEN

THE fumes of my resentment being dissipated, as well as the vanity of my success, I found myself deserted to all the horrors of extreme want, and avoided by mankind as a creature of a different species, or rather as a solitary being, no ways comprehended within the scheme or protection of Providence. My despair had rendered me almost quite stupefied, when I was one day told that a gentleman desired to see me at a certain public-house, whither immediately I repaired, and was introduced to one Mr. Launcelot Crab, a surgeon in town, who was engaged with two more in drinking a liquor called *pop-in*, composed by mixing a quartern of brandy with a quart of small beer. Before I relate the occasion of this message, I believe it will not be disagreeable to the reader if I describe the gentleman who sent for me, and mention some circumstances of his character and conduct, which may illustrate what follows, and account for his behavior to me.

This member of the faculty was aged fifty, about five feet high, and ten round the belly; his face was capacious as a full moon, and much of the complexion of a mulberry; his nose, resembling a powder-horn, was swelled to an enormous size, and studded all over with carbuncles; and his little gray eyes reflected the rays in such an oblique manner, that, while he looked a person full in the face, one would have imagined he was admiring the buckle of his shoe. He had long entertained an implacable resentment against Potion, who, though a young practitioner, was better employed than he, and once had the assurance to perform a cure whereby he disappointed and disgraced the prognostic of the said Crab. This quarrel, which was at one time upon the point of being made up by the interposition and mediation of friends, had been lately inflamed beyond a possibility of reconciliation by the respective wives of the opponents, who, chancing to meet at a christening, disagreed about precedence, proceeded from invectives to blows, and were, with great difficulty, by the gossips, prevented from converting the occasion of joy into a scene of lamentation.

The difference between these rivals was in the height of rancor, when I received the message of Crab, who received me as civilly as I could have expected from one of his disposition; and, after desiring me to sit, inquired into the particulars of my leaving the house of Potion; which, when I had related, he said with a malicious grin, "There's a sneaking dog!—I always thought him a fellow without a soul, d—n me!—a canting scoundrel, who has crept into business by his hypocrisy, and kissing the a—se of everybody."

"Aye, aye," says another, "one might see with half an eye that the rascal has no honesty in him, by his going so regularly to church." This sentence was confirmed by a third, who assured his companions, that Potion was never known to be disguised in liquor but once, at a meeting of the godly, where he had distinguished himself by an *extempore* prayer an hour long. After this preamble, Crab addressed himself to me in these words: "Well, my lad, I have heard a good character of you, and I'll do for you. You may send your things to my house when you please. I have given orders for your reception. Zounds! what does the booby stare at?—If you have no mind to embrace my courteous offer, you may let it alone, and be d—d." I answered, with a submissive bow, that I was far from rejecting his friendly offer, which I would immediately accept, as soon as he should inform me on what footing I was to be entertained. "What footing! d—n my blood," cried he; "d'ye expect to have a footman and a couple of horses kept for you?" "No, sir," I replied, "my expectations are not quite so sanguine. That I may be as little burdensome as possible, I would willingly serve in your shop, by which means I may save you the expense of a journeyman, or porter at least, for I understand a little pharmacy, having employed some of my leisure hours in the practice of that art while I lived with Mr. Potion: neither am I altogether ignorant of surgery, which I have studied with great pleasure and application." "Oho! you did?" says Crab. "Gentlemen, here

is a complete artist!—Studied surgery! what?
in books, I suppose. I shall have you disput-
ing with me one of these days on points of my
profession. You can already account for muscu-
lar motion, I warrant, and explain the mystery
of the brain and nerves—ha? You are too
learned for me, d—n me. But let's hear no more
of this stuff. Can you bleed and give a clyster,
spread a plaster, and prepare a potion?'' Upon
my answering in the affirmative he shook his
head, telling me he believed he should have little
good of me, for all my promises; but, however,
he would take me in for the sake of charity.

I was accordingly that very night admitted to
his house, and had an apartment assigned to
me in the garret, which I was fain to put up with,
notwithstanding the mortification my pride suffered in this change of circumstances. I was soon
convinced of the real motives which induced Crab
to receive me in this manner: for, besides the
gratification of his revenge, by exposing the selfishness of his antagonist in opposition to his own
generosity, which was all affectation, he had occasion for a young man who understood something of the profession, to fill up the place of
his eldest apprentice, lately dead, not without violent suspicion of foul play from his master's brutality. The knowledge of this circumstance, together with his daily behavior to his wife and the
young apprentice, did not at all contribute to
my enjoying my new situation with ease; however, as I did not perceive how I could bestow myself to better advantage, I resolved to study

Crab's temper with all the application, and manage it with all the address, in my power. And it was not long before I found out a strange peculiarity of humor, which governed his behavior toward all his dependents. I observed, when he was pleased, he was such a niggard of his satisfaction, that, if his wife or servants betrayed the least symptom of participation, he was offended to an insupportable degree of choler and fury, the effects of which they seldom failed to feel. And, when his indignation was roused, submission and soothing always exasperated it beyond the bounds of reason and humanity. I therefore pursued a contrary plan; and one day, when he honored me with the names of ignorant whelp, and lazy ragamuffin, I boldly replied, "I was neither ignorant nor lazy, since I both understood and performed my business as well as he could do for his soul; neither was it just to call me ragamuffin, for I had a whole coat on my back, and was descended from a better family than any he could boast an alliance with." He gave tokens of great amazement at this assurance of mine, and shook his cane over my head, regarding me all the time with a countenance truly diabolical. Although I was terribly startled at his menacing looks and posture, I yet had reflection enough left to convince me I had gone too far to retract, and that this was the critical minute which must decide my future lot in his service; I therefore snatched up the pestle of a mortar, and swore, if he offered to strike me without a cause, I should see whether his skull or my weapon was hardest.

He continued silent for some time, and at last broke forth into these ejaculations: "This is fine usage from a servant to a master,—very fine!—d—tion!—but no matter, you shall pay for this, you dog, you shall. I'll do your business—yes, yes, I'll teach you to lift your hand against me." So saying, he retired, and left me under dreadful apprehensions, which vanished entirely at our next meeting, when he behaved with unusual complacency, and treated me with a glass of punch after dinner. By this conduct I got the ascendency over him in a short time, and became so necessary to him, in managing his business while he was engaged at the bottle, that fortune began to wear a kinder aspect; and I consoled myself for the disregard of my former acquaintance with the knowledge I daily imbibed, by a close application to the duties of my employment, in which I succeeded beyond my own expectations. I was on very good terms with my master's wife, whose esteem I acquired and cultivated, by representing Mrs. Potion in the most ridiculous lights my satirical talents could invent, as well as by rendering her some Christian offices when she had been too familiar with the dram bottle, to which she had oftentimes recourse for consolation under the affliction she suffered from her barbarous husband.

In this manner I lived, without hearing the least tidings of my uncle, for the space of two years, during which time I kept little or no company, being neither in a humor to relish, nor in a capacity to maintain much acquaintance: for the

Nabal, my master, allowed me no wages; and the small perquisites of my station scarce supplied me with the common necessaries of life. I was no longer a pert, unthinking coxcomb, giddy with popular applause, and elevated with the extravagance of hope: my misfortunes had taught me how little the caresses of the world, during a man's prosperity, are to be valued by him; and how seriously and expeditiously he ought to set about making himself independent of them. My present appearance, therefore, was the least of my care, which was wholly engrossed in laying up a stock of instruction that might secure me against the caprice of fortune for the future. I became such a sloven, and contracted such an air of austerity, that everybody pronounced me crestfallen; and Gawky returned to town, without running any risk from my resentment, which was by this time pretty much cooled, and restrained by the prudential reasons so effectually, that I never so much as thought of obtaining satisfaction for the injuries he had done me. When I deemed myself sufficiently master of my business, I began to cast about for an opportunity of launching into the world, in hope of finding some provision that might make amends for the difficulties I had undergone: but, as this could not be effected without a small sum of money to equip me for the field, I was in the utmost perplexity how to raise it, well knowing that Crab, for his own sake, would never put me in a condition to leave him, when his interest was so much concerned in my stay. But a small accident which happened

I—4

about this time determined him in my favor. This was no other than the pregnancy of his maid-servant, who declared her situation to me, assuring me, at the same time, that I was the occasion of it. Although I had no reason to question the truth of this imputation, I was not ignorant of the familiarities which had passed between her master and her; taking the advantage of which I represented to her the folly of laying the burden at my door, when she might dispose of it to much better purpose with Mr. Crab. She listened to my advice, and next day acquainted him with the pretended success of their mutual endeavors. He was far from being overjoyed at this proof of his vigor, which he foresaw might have very troublesome consequences; not that he dreaded any domestic grumblings and reproaches from his wife, whom he kept in perfect subjection; but because he knew it would furnish his rival Potion with a handle for insulting and undermining his reputation; there being no scandal equal to that of uncleanliness in the opinion of those who inhabit the part of the island where he lived. He, therefore, took a resolution worthy of himself; which was, to persuade the girl that she was not with child, but only afflicted with a disorder incident to young women, which he would easily remove. With this view, as he pretended, he prescribed for her such medicines as he thought would infallibly procure abortion; but in this scheme he was disappointed; for the maid, being advertised by me of his design, and at the same time well acquainted with her own condi-

tion, absolutely refused to follow his directions;
and threatened to publish her situation to the
world, if he would not immediately take some
method of providing for the important occasion,
which she expected in a few months. It was not
long before I guessed the result of his deliberation, by his addressing himself to me, one day,
in this manner: "I am surprised that a young
fellow like you discovers no inclination to push
his fortune in the world. Before I was of your
age I was broiling on the coast of Guinea.—D—
me! what's to hinder you from profiting by the
war which will certainly be declared in a short
time against Spain? You may easily get on
board of a king's ship in quality of a surgeon's
mate; where you will certainly see a great deal
of practice, and stand a good chance of getting
prize-money." I laid hold of this declaration,
which I had long wished for, and assured him I
would follow his advice with pleasure, if it was
in my power; but that it was impossible for me
to embrace an opportunity of that kind, as I had
no friend to advance a little money to supply me
with what necessaries I should want, and defray
the expenses of my journey to London. He told
me that few necessaries were required; and as for
the expense of my journey, he would lend me
money sufficient not only for that purpose, but
also to maintain me comfortably in London until
I should procure a warrant for my provision on
board of some ship. I gave him a thousand thanks
for his obliging offer (although I was very well
apprised of his motive, which was no other than

a design to lay the bastard to my charge after my departure), and accordingly set out in a few weeks for London, my whole fortune consisting of one suit of clothes, half a dozen of ruffled shirts, as many plain, two pair of worsted, and a like number of thread stockings, a case of pocket instruments, a small edition of Horace, Wiseman's Surgery, and ten guineas in cash, for which Crab took my bond, bearing five per cent. interest; at the same time [he] gave me a letter to the member of parliament for our town, which, he said, would do my business effectually.

CHAPTER EIGHT

THERE is no such convenience as a wagon
in this country, and my finances were too
weak to support the expense of hiring a
horse; I determined therefore to set out with the
carriers, who transport goods from one place to
another on horseback; and this scheme I accordingly put in execution on the first day of No-
vember 1739, sitting upon a pack-saddle between
two baskets, one of which contained my goods
in a knapsack. But, by the time we arrived at
Newcastle-upon-Tyne, I was so fatigued with the
tediousness of the carriage, and benumbed with
the coldness of the weather, that I resolved to
travel the rest of my journey on foot, rather than
proceed in such a disagreeable manner.

The hostler of the inn at which we put up, understanding I was bound for London, advised me
to take my passage in a collier, which would be
both cheap and expeditious, and withal much
easier than to walk upward of three hundred
miles through deep roads in the winter time; a
journey which, he believed, I had not strength
enough to perform. I was almost persuaded to

take his advice, when, one day, stepping into a
barber's shop to be shaved, the young man, while
he lathered my face, accosted me thus: "Sir, I
presume you are a Scotchman." I answered in
the affirmative. "Pray," continued he, "from
what part of Scotland?"—I no sooner told him,
than he discovered great emotion, and not confin-
ing his operation to my chin and upper lip, besmeared my whole face with great agitation. I
was so offended at this profusion, that, starting
up, I asked him what the d—l he meant by using
me so? He begged pardon, telling me his joy
at meeting with a countryman had occasioned
some confusion in him; and craved my name.
But when I declared my name was Random, he
exclaimed in a rapture, "How! Rory Random?"
The same, I replied, looking at him with astonishment. "What," cried he, "don't you know
your old schoolfellow, Hugh Strap?" At that
instant, recollecting his face, I flew into his arms,
and in the transport of my joy, gave him back
one half of the suds he had so lavishly bestowed
on my countenance; so that we made a very ludicrous appearance, and furnished a great deal of
mirth for his master and shopmates, who were
witnesses of this scene. When our mutual caresses were over, I sat down again to be shaved;
but the poor fellow's nerves were so discomposed
by this unexpected meeting, that his hand could
scarcely hold the razor, with which, nevertheless,
he found means to cut me in three places, in as
many strokes. His master, perceiving his disorder, bade another supply his place, and after the

operation was performed, gave Strap leave to
pass the rest of the day with me. We retired immediately to my lodgings, where, calling for some
beer, I desired to be informed of his adventures,
which contained nothing more, than that his master dying before his time was out, he had come
to Newcastle about a year ago, in expectation of
journey-work, along with three young fellows of
his acquaintance, who worked in the keels; that
he had the good fortune of being employed by a
very civil master, with whom he intended to stay
till the spring, at which time he proposed to go
to London, where he did not doubt of finding encouragement. When I communicated to him my
situation and design, he did not approve of my
taking a passage by sea, by reason of the danger
of a winter voyage, which is very hazardous along
that coast, as well as the precariousness of the
wind, which might possibly detain me a great
while, to the no small detriment of my fortune.
Whereas, if I would venture by land, he would
bear me company, carry my baggage all the way,
and, if we should be fatigued before we could
perform all the journey, it would be no hard matter for us to find on the road either returning
horses or wagons, of which we might take the advantage for a very trifling expense. I was so
ravished at this proposal, that I embraced him
affectionately, and assured him he might command my purse to the last farthing: but he gave
me to understand, he had saved money sufficient
to answer his own occasions; and that he had a
friend in London, who would soon introduce him

into business in that capital, and might possibly
have it in his power to serve me also.

Having concerted the plan and settled our affairs that night, we departed next morning by
daybreak, armed with a good cudgel each (my
companion being charged with the furniture of us
both, crammed into one knapsack), and our money
sewed between the lining and waistband of our
breeches, except some loose silver for our immediate expense on the road. We traveled all day
at a round pace, but, being ignorant of the proper
stages, were benighted at a good distance from
any inn, so that we were compelled to take up
our lodging at a small hedge ale-house, that stood
on a by-road, about half a mile from the highway.
There we found a peddler of our own country, in
whose company we regaled ourselves with bacon
and eggs, and a glass of good ale, before a comfortable fire, conversing all the while very so-
ciably with the landlord and his daughter, an hale
buxom lass, who entertained us with great good
humor, and in whose affection I was vain enough
to believe I had made some progress. About
eight o'clock, we were all three, at our own desire,
shown into an apartment, furnished with two
beds, in one of which Strap and I betook ourselves
to rest, and the peddler occupied the other, though
not before he had prayed a considerable time *extempore,* searched into every corner of the room,
and fastened the door on the inside with a strong
iron screw, which he carried about with him for
that use. I slept very sound till midnight, when
I was disturbed by a violent motion of the bed,

which shook under me with a continual tremor. Alarmed at this phenomenon, I jogged my companion, whom, to my no small amazement, I found drenched in sweat, and quaking through every limb; he told me, with a low faltering voice, that we were undone; for there was a bloody highwayman loaded with pistols in the next room; then bidding me make as little noise as possible, he directed me to a small chink in the board partition, through which I could see a thick-set brawny fellow, with a fierce countenance, sitting at a table with our young landlady, having a bottle of ale and a brace of pistols before him. I listened with great attention, and heard him say in a terrible tone: "D—n that son of a bitch, Smack, the coachman;—he has served me a fine trick, indeed!—but d—tion seize me, if I don't make him repent it! I'll teach the scoundrel to give intelligence to others, while he is under articles with me."

Our landlady endeavored to appease this exasperated robber, by saying he might be mistaken in Smack, who perhaps kept no correspondence with the other gentleman that robbed his coach; and that, if an accident had disappointed him today, he might soon find opportunity enough to atone for his lost trouble. "I'll tell thee what, my dear Bett," replied he, "I never had, nor ever will, while my name is Rifle, have such a glorious booty as I missed to-day.—Zounds! there was four hundred pounds in cash to recruit men for the king's service, besides the jewels, watches, swords, and money belonging to the passengers;

—had it been my fortune to have got clear off
with so much treasure, I would have purchased
a commission in the army, and made you an officer's lady, you jade, I would." "Well, well,"
cries Betty, "we must trust to Providence for
that;—but did you find nothing worth taking,
which escaped the other gentleman of the road?"
"Not much, faith," said the lover; "I gleaned a
few things, such as a pair of pops, silver mounted,
(here they are); I took them loaded from the
captain who had the charge of the money, together with a gold watch, which he had concealed
in his breeches. I likewise found ten Portugal
pieces in the shoes of a Quaker, whom the spirit
moved to revile me with great bitterness and devotion. But what I value myself mostly for, is
this here purchase, a gold snuff-box, my girl, with
a picture on the inside of the lid; which I untied
out of the tail of a pretty lady's smock." Here,
as the devil would have it, the peddler snored so
loud, that the highwayman, snatching his pistols,
started up, crying: "Hell and d—tion! I am
betrayed; who's that in the next room?" Mrs.
Betty told him, he need not be uneasy; there were
only three poor wearied travelers, who, missing
the road, had taken up their lodging in the house,
and were asleep long ago. "Travelers?" says
he, "spies, you b—ch! but no matter—I'll send
them all to hell in an instant." He accordingly
ran toward our door; when his sweetheart interposing, assured him, there was only a couple of
poor young Scotchmen, who were too raw and ig-

norant to give him the least cause of suspicion;
and the third was a Presbyterian peddler of the
same nation, who had often lodged in the house
before. This declaration satisfied the thief, who
swore he was glad there was a peddler, for he
wanted some linen. Then, in a jovial manner, he
put about the glass, mingling his discourse to
Betty with caresses and familiarities that spoke
him very happy in his amours. During that part
of the conversation which regarded us, Strap had
crept under the bed, where he lay in the agonies
of fear; so that it was with great difficulty I persuaded him our danger was over, and prevailed
on him to wake the peddler, and inform him of
what he had seen and heard. This itinerant merchant no sooner felt somebody shaking him by
the shoulder, than he started up, calling as loud
as he could, "Thieves! thieves! Lord have mercy
on us!" And Rifle, alarmed at this exclamation,
jumped up, cocked one of his pistols, and turned
toward the door, to kill the first man who should
enter; for he verily believed himself beset; when
his Dulcinea, after an immoderate fit of laughter,
persuaded him, that the poor peddler, dreaming of
thieves, had only cried out in his sleep. Meanwhile my comrade had undeceived our fellow-
lodger, and informed him of his reason for dis-
turbing him; upon which, getting up softly, he
peeped through the hole, and was so terrified with
what he saw, that, falling down on his bare knees,
he put up a long petition to Heaven, to deliver
him from the hands of that ruffian, and promised

never to defraud a customer for the future of the value of a pin's point, provided he might be rescued from the present danger.

Whether or not his disburdening his conscience afforded him any ease, I know not; but he slipped into bed again, and lay very quiet until the robber and his mistress were asleep, and snored in concert; then, rising softly, he untied a rope that was round his pack, which making fast to one end of it, he opened the window with as little noise as possible, and lowered his goods into the yard with great dexterity; then he moved gently to our bedside, and bade us farewell, telling us, that, as we ran no risk, we might take our rest with great confidence, and in the morning assure the landlord that we knew nothing of his escape; and lastly, shaking us by the hands, and wishing us all manner of success, he let himself drop from the window without any danger, for the ground was not above a yard from his feet as he hung on the outside. Although I did not think proper to accompany him in his flight, I was not at all free from apprehension, when I reflected on what might be the effect of the highwayman's disappointment, as he certainly intended to make free with the peddler's ware. Neither was my companion at more ease in his mind; but, on the contrary, so possessed with the dreadful idea of Rifle, that he solicited me strongly to follow our countryman's example, and so elude the fatal resentment of that terrible adventurer, who would certainly wreak his vengeance on us, as accomplices of the peddler's elopement. But I repre-

sented to him the danger of giving Rifle cause to
think we knew his profession, and suggested that,
if ever he should meet us again on the road, he
would look upon us as dangerous acquaintance,
and find it his interest to put us out of the way.
I told him withal my confidence in Betty's good
nature, in which he acquiesced; and, during the
remaining part of the night, we concerted a
proper method of behavior, to render us unsus-
pected in the morning.

It was no sooner day, than Betty, entering our
chamber, and perceiving our window open, cried
out: "Ods bobs! sure you Scotchmen must have
hot constitutions to lie all night with the window
open, in such cold weather." I feigned to start
out of sleep, and withdrawing the curtain, called,
"What's the matter?" When she showed me, I
affected surprise, and said, "Bless me! the window was shut when we went to bed." "I'll be
hanged," said she, "if Sawney Waddle the peddler has not got up in a dream and done it, for I
heard him very obstropulous in his sleep.—Sure
I put a chamber-pot under his bed." With these
words she advanced to the bed in which he lay,
and finding the sheets cold, exclaimed, "Good
lack-a-daisy! the rogue is fled!" "Fled!" cried
I, with feigned amazement, "God forbid!—Sure
he has not robbed us." Then springing up, I laid
hold of my breeches, and emptied all my loose
money into my hand; which having reckoned, I
said, "Heaven be praised, our money is all safe:
—Strap, look to the knapsack." He did so, and
found all was right. Upon which we asked, with

seeming concern, if he had stole nothing belonging to the house? "No, no," replied she, "he has stole nothing but his reckoning"; which, it seems, this pious peddler had forgot to discharge, in the midst of his devotion. Betty, after a moment's pause, withdrew; and immediately we could hear her waken Rifle, who no sooner heard of Waddle's flight, than he jumped out of bed, and dressed, venting a thousand execrations, and vowing to murder the peddler, if ever he should set eyes on him again: "For," said he, "the scoundrel has by this time raised the hue and cry against me." Having dressed himself in a hurry, he mounted his horse, and for that time rid us of his company, and a thousand fears that were the consequence of it. While we were at breakfast, Betty endeavored, by all the cunning she was mistress of, to learn whether or no we suspected our fellow-lodger, whom we saw take horse; but as we were on our guard, we answered her sly questions with a simplicity she could not distrust; when, all of a sudden, we heard the trampling of a horse's feet at the door.

This noise alarmed Strap so much, whose imagination was wholly engrossed by the image of Rifle, that, with a countenance as pale as milk, he cried, "O Lord! there's the highwayman returned!" Our landlady, staring at these words, said, "What highwayman, young man?—Do you think any highwaymen harbor here?" Though I was very much disconcerted at this piece of indiscretion in Strap, I had presence of mind enough to tell her, we had met a horseman the day

before, whom Strap had foolishly supposed to be
a highwayman, because he rode with pistols; and
that he had been terrified at the sound of a horse's
feet ever since. She forced a smile at the ignorance and timidity of my comrade; but I could
perceive (not without great concern) that this
account was not at all satisfactory to her.

CHAPTER NINE

We proceed on our Journey—Are overtaken by an Highwayman, who fires at Strap—Is prevented from shooting
me by a Company of Horsemen, who ride in pursuit of
him—Strap is put to Bed at an Inn—Adventures at that
inn.

AFTER having paid our score, and taken
leave of our hostess, who embraced me
tenderly at parting, we proceeded on our
journey, blessing ourselves that we had come off
so well. We had not walked above five miles,
when we observed a man on horseback galloping
after us, whom we in a short time recognized to
be no other than this formidable hero who had
already given us so much vexation. He stopped
hard by me, and asked if I knew who he was?
My astonishment had disconcerted me so much,
that I did not hear his question, which he repeated with a volley of oaths and threats; but I
remained as mute as before. Strap seeing my
discomposure, fell upon his knees in the mud,
uttering with a lamentable voice these words:
"For Christ's sake, have mercy upon us, Mr.
Rifle,—we know you very well." "Oho!" cried
the thief, "you do!—but you never shall be evidence against me in this world, you dog!" So
saying, he drew a pistol, and fired it at the unfortunate shaver, who fell flat upon the ground,

without speaking one word. My comrade's fate, and my own situation, riveted me to the place where I stood, deprived of all sense and reflection; so that I did not make the least attempt either to run away, or deprecate the wrath of this barbarian, who snapped a second pistol at me; but before he had time to prime again, perceiving a company of horsemen coming up, he rode off, and left me standing motionless as a statue, in which posture I was found by those whose appearance had saved my life.

This company consisted of three men in livery, well armed, with an officer, who, as I afterward learned, was the person from whom Rifle had taken the pocket-pistols the day before; and who, making known his misfortune to a nobleman he met on the road, and assuring him his non-resistance was altogether owing to his consideration for the ladies in the coach, procured the assistance of his lordship's servants to go in quest of the plunderer. This holiday captain scampered up to me with great address, and asked who fired the pistol which he had heard. As I had not yet recovered my reason, he, before I could answer, observed a body lying on the ground: at which sight his color changed, and he pronounced with a faltering tongue, "Gentlemen, here's murder committed! Let us alight." "No, no," said one of his followers, "let us rather pursue the murderer. Which way went he, young man?" By this time I had recollected myself so far as to tell them, that he could not be a quarter of a mile before; and to beg of one of them to

I—5

assist me in conveying the corpse of my friend
to the next house, in order to its being interred.
The captain, foreseeing, that, in case he should
pursue, he must soon come to action, began to
curb his horse, and give him the spur at the same
time, which treatment making the creature rear
up and snort, he called out, his horse was frightened, and would not proceed; at the same time
wheeling him round and round, stroking his neck,
whistling and wheeling him with "Sirrah, sirrah,
gently, gently, etc."—"Zounds!" cried one of the
servants, "sure my lord's Sorrel is not resty!"—
With these words, he bestowed a lash on his but-
tocks, and Sorrel, disdaining the rein, sprung forward with the captain at a pace that would have
soon brought him up with the robber, had not the
girth, happily for him, given way, by which means
he landed in the dirt; and two of his attendants
continued their pursuit, without minding his situation. Meanwhile, one of the three who remained at my desire, turning the body of Strap,
in order to see the wound which had killed him,
found him still warm, and breathing; upon which
I immediately let him blood, and saw him, with
inexpressible joy, recover; he having received no
other wound than what his fear had inflicted.
Having raised him upon his legs, we walked together to an inn, about half a mile from the place,
where Strap, who was not quite recovered, went
to bed; and in a little time, the third servant
returned with the captain's horse and furniture,
leaving him to crawl after as well as he could.
This gentleman of the sword, upon his arrival,

complained grievously of the bruise occasioned by his fall; and, on the recommendation of the servant, who warranted my ability, I was employed to bleed him, for which service he rewarded me with half a crown.

The time between this event and dinner, I passed in observing a game at cards between two farmers, an exciseman, and a young fellow in a rusty gown and cassock, who, as I afterward understood, was curate of a neighboring parish. It was easy to perceive, that the match was not equal; and that the two farmers, who were partners, had to do with a couple of sharpers, who stripped them of all their cash in a very short time. But what surprised me very much was, to hear this clergyman reply to one of the countrymen who seemed to suspect foul play, in these words: "D—n me, friend, d'ye question my honor?"—I did not at all wonder to find a cheat in canonicals, this being a character frequent in my own country; but I was scandalized at the indecency of his behavior, which appeared in the oaths he swore, and the bawdy songs which he sung. At last, to make amends, in some sort, for the damage he had done to the unwary boors, he pulled out a fiddle from the lining of his gown, and, promising to treat them at dinner, began to play most melodiously, singing in concert all the while. This good humor of the parson inspired the company with so much glee, that the farmers soon forgot their losses, and all present went to dancing in the yard. While we were agreeably amused in this manner, our musician,

spying a horseman riding toward the inn, stopped
all of a sudden, crying out, "Gad so! gentlemen,
I beg your pardon; there's our dog of a doctor
coming into the inn." He immediately concealed
his instrument, and ran toward the gate, where
he took hold of the vicar's bridle, and helped him
off, inquiring very cordially into the state of his
health. This rosy son of the church, who might
be about the age of fifty, having alighted, and
entrusted the curate with his horse, stalked with
great solemnity into the kitchen, where, sitting
down by the fire, he called for a bottle of ale
and a pipe; scarce deigning an answer to the submissive questions of those who inquired about
the welfare of his family. While he indulged
himself in this state, amidst a profound silence,
the curate, approaching him with great reverence,
asked if he would not be pleased to honor us with
his company at dinner? To which interrogation
he answered in the negative, saying, he had been
to visit Squire Bumpkin, who had drank himself
into a high fever at the last assizes; and that he
had, on leaving his own house, told Betty he
should dine at home. Accordingly, when he had
made an end of his bottle and pipe, he rose and
moved, with prelatical dignity, to the door, where
his journeyman stood ready with his nag. He
had no sooner mounted, than the facetious curate,
coming into the kitchen, held forth in this manner: "There the old rascal goes, and the devil
go with him.—You see how the world wags, gentlemen.—By gad, this rogue of a vicar does not
deserve to live; and yet he has two livings worth

£400 per annum, while poor I am fain to do all his drudgery, and ride twenty miles every Sunday to preach, for what? why, truly, for £20 a year. I scorn to boast of my own qualifications; but—comparisons are odious. I should be glad to know how this swag-bellied doctor deserves to be more at ease than me. He can loll in his elbow-chair at home, indulge himself in the best of vict-uals and wine, and enjoy the conversation of Betty, his housekeeper. You understand me, gen-tlemen. Betty is the doctor's poor kinswoman, and a pretty girl she is; but no matter for that: —ay, and a dutiful girl to her parents, whom she visits regularly every year, though I must own, I could never learn in what county they live.— My service t'ye, gentlemen."

By this time dinner being ready, I waked my companion, and we ate all together with great cheerfulness. When our meal was ended, and every man's share of the reckoning adjusted, the curate went out on pretense of some necessary occasion, and mounting his horse, left the two farmers to satisfy the host in the best manner they could. We were no sooner informed of this piece of finesse, than the exciseman, who had been silent hitherto, began to open with a malicious grin: "Ay, ay, this is an old trick of Shuffle: I could not help smiling when he talked of treat-ing. You must know this is a very curious fel-low. He picked up some scraps of learning while he served young Lord Trifle at the university. But what he most excels in is pimping. No man knows his talents better than I; for I was valet

de chambre to Squire Tattle, an intimate companion of Shuffle's lord. He got himself into a
scrape, by pawning some of his lordship's clothes,
on which account he was turned away; but, as
he was acquainted with some particular circumstances of my lord's conduct, he did not care to
exasperate him too much, and so made interest
for his receiving orders, and afterward recommended him to the curacy which he now enjoys.
However, the fellow cannot be too much admired
for his dexterity in making a comfortable liveli-
hood, in spite of such a small allowance. You
hear he plays a good stick, and is really diverting
in company. These qualifications make him
agreeable wherever he goes; and, as for playing
at cards, there is not a man within three counties
a match for him: the truth is, he is a damnable
cheat; and can shift a card with such address,
that it is impossible to discover him." Here he
was interrupted by one of the farmers, who asked
why he had not justice enough to acquaint them
with these particulars before they engaged in
play? The exciseman replied, without any hesitation, that it was none of his business to in-
termeddle between man and man; besides, he did
not know they were ignorant of Shuffle's character, which was notorious to the whole country.
This did not satisfy the other, who taxed him with
abetting and assisting the curate's knavery, and
insisted on having his share of the winnings returned; this demand the exciseman as positively
refused, affirming, that whatsoever sleights Shuffle might practice on other occasions, he was very

certain that he had played on the square with
them, and would answer it before any bench in
Christendom; so saying, he got up, and having
paid his reckoning, sneaked off. The landlord
thrusting his neck into the passage, to see if he
was gone, shook his head, saying, "Ah! Lord help
us, if every sinner was to have his deserts.—Well,
we victualers must not disoblige the exciseman.
—But I know what:—if parson Shuffle and he
were weighed together, a straw thrown into either
scale would make the balance kick the beam.—
But, masters, this is under the rose," continued
Boniface, with a whisper.

CHAPTER TEN

STRAP and I were about to depart on our
journey, when we perceived a crowd on the
road coming toward us, shouting and hal-
looing all the way. As it approached, we could
discern a man on horseback in the middle, with
his hands tied behind him, whom we soon knew
to be Rifle. This highwayman, not being so well
mounted as the two servants who went in pursuit
of him, was soon overtaken, and, after having discharged his pistols, made prisoner without any
further opposition. They were carrying him in
triumph, amidst the acclamations of the country
people, to a justice of peace in a neighboring village, but stopped at our inn to join their companion, and take refreshment. When Rifle was dis-
mounted, and placed in the yard, within a circle
of peasants armed with pitchforks, I was amazed
to see what a pitiful dejected fellow he now appeared, who had but a few hours before filled me
with such terror and confusion. My companion
was so much encouraged by this alteration in his
appearance, that, going up to the thief, he pre-

sented his clenched fists to his nose, and declared
he would either cudgel or box with the prisoner
for a guinea, which he immediately produced, and
began to strip, but was dissuaded from his adventure by me, who represented to him the folly
of the undertaking, as Rifle was now in the hands
of justice, which would, no doubt, give us all satisfaction enough. But what made me repent of
our impertinent curiosity, was our being detained
by the captors as evidence against him, when we
were just going to set forward. However, there
was no remedy; we were obliged to comply; and
accordingly joined in the cavalcade, which luckily
took the same road that we had proposed to follow.

About the twilight we arrived at the place of
our destination; but, as the justice was gone to
visit a gentleman in the country, with whom, we
understood, he would probably stay all night, the
robber was confined in an empty garret three
stories high, from which it seemed impossible for
him to escape. This, nevertheless, was the case;
for next morning, when they went upstairs to
bring him before the justice, the bird was flown,
having got out at the window upon the roof, from
whence he continued his route along the tops of
the adjoining houses, and entered another garret
window, where he skulked until the family were
asleep, at which time he ventured downstairs, and
let himself out by the street door, which was found
open. This event was a great disappointment to
those that apprehended him, who were flushed
with hopes of the reward; but gave me great joy,

as I was permitted now to continue my journey without any further molestation. Resolving to make up for the small progress we had hitherto made, we this day traveled with great vigor, and before night reached a market-town, twenty miles from the place from whence we set out in the morning, without meeting any adventure worth notice. Here having taken up our lodging at an inn, I found myself so fatigued, that I began to despair of performing our journey on foot, and desired Strap to inquire if there were any wagon, return-horses, or other cheap carriage in this place, to depart for London next day. He was informed, that the wagon from Newcastle to London had halted there two nights ago; and that it would be an easy matter to overtake it, if not the next day, at farthest the day after the next. This piece of news gave us some satisfaction; and, after having made a hearty supper on hashed mutton, we were shown to our room, which contained two beds, the one allotted for us, and the other for a very honest gentleman, who, we were told, was then drinking below. Though we could have very well dispensed with his company, we were glad to submit to this disposition, as there was not another bed empty in the house; and accordingly went to rest, after having secured our baggage under the bolster.

About two or three o'clock in the morning, I was waked out of a very profound sleep, by a dreadful noise in the chamber, which did not fail to throw me into an agony of consternation, when I heard these words pronounced with a terrible voice: "Blood and wounds! run the halbert into the guts of him that's next you, and I'll blow the other's brains out presently." This dreadful salutation had no sooner reached the ears of Strap, than, starting out of bed, he ran against somebody in the dark, and overturned him in an instant; at the same time bawling out, "Fire! murder! fire!" a cry which in a moment alarmed the whole house, and filled our chamber with a crowd of naked people. When lights were brought, the occasion of all this disturbance soon appeared; which was no other than our fellow-lodger, whom we found lying on the floor scratching his head, with a look testifying the utmost astonishment at the concourse of apparitions that surrounded him.—This honest gentleman was, it seems, a recruiting sergeant, who, having listed two country fellows overnight, dreamed they had mutinied, and threatened to murder him and the drummer who was along with him. This made such an impression on his imagination, that he got up in his sleep, and expressed himself as above.

When our apprehension of danger vanished, the company beheld one another with great surprise and mirth; but what attracted the notice of every one, was our landlady, with nothing on her but her shift, and a large pair of buckskin breeches, with the backside before, which she had slipt on in the hurry, and her husband, with her petticoat about his shoulders. One had wrapped himself in a blanket, another was covered with a sheet, and the drummer, who had given his only shirt to be washed, appeared in cuerpo, with the bolster

rolled about his middle. When this affair was
discussed, everybody retired to his own apartment, the sergeant slipped into bed, and my companion and I slept without any further disturbance till morning, when we got up, went to
breakfast, paid our reckoning, and set forward,
in expectation of overtaking the wagon; in which
hope, however, we were disappointed for that day.
As we exerted ourselves more than usual, I found
myself quite spent with fatigue, when we entered
a small village in the twilight. We inquired for
a public-house, and were directed to one of a very
sorry appearance. At our entrance, the landlord,
who seemed to be a venerable old man, with long
gray hair, rose from a table placed by a large
fire in a very neat paved kitchen, and, with a
cheerful countenance, accosted us in these words:
"Salvete, pueri, ingredimini." I was not a little
pleased to hear our host speak Latin, because
I was in hope of recommending myself to him by
my knowledge in that language; I therefore answered, without hesitation,—*"Dissolve frigus,
ligna super foco—large reponens."* I had no
sooner pronounced these words, than the old gentleman, running toward me, shook me by the hand,
crying, *"Fili mi dilectissime! unde venis? a su-
peris, ni fallor!"* In short, finding we were both
read in the classics, he did not know how to tes-
tify his regard enough; but ordered his daughter,
a jolly, rosy-cheeked damsel, who was his sole
domestic, to bring us a bottle of his *quadrimum*,
repeating from Horace at the same time, *"De-
prome quadrimum Sabina, O Thaliarche, merum*

diota." This *quadrimum* was excellent ale of his own brewing, of which he told us he had always an *amphora* four years old for the use of himself and friends. In the course of our conversation, which was interlarded with scraps of Latin, we understood that this facetious person was a schoolmaster, whose income being small, he was fain to keep a glass of good liquor for the entertainment of passengers, by which he made shift to make the two ends of the year meet. "I am this day," said he, "the happiest old fellow in his Majesty's dominions. My wife, rest her soul, is in heaven. My daughter is to be married next week; but the two chief pleasures of my life are these (pointing to the bottle and a large edition of Horace that lay on the table). I am old, 'tis true,—what then? the more reason I should enjoy the small share of life that remains, as my friend Flaccus advises: *'Tu ne quæsieris (scire nefas) quem mihi, quem tibi finem di dederint. Carpe diem, quam minimum credula postero.'*"

As he was very inquisitive about our affairs, we made no scruple of acquainting him with our situation, which when he had learned, he enriched us with advices how to behave in the world, telling us, that he was no stranger to the deceits of mankind. In the meantime, he ordered his daughter to lay a fowl to the fire for supper, for he was resolved this night to regale his friends—*permittens divis cætera.* While our entertainment was preparing, our host recounted the adventures of his own life, which, as they contain nothing remarkable, I forbear to rehearse. When we had

fared sumptuously, and drank several bottles of
his *quadrimum*, I expressed a desire of going to
rest, which was with some difficulty complied with,
after he had informed us, that we should overtake the wagon by noon next day; and that there
was room enough in it for half a dozen, for there
were only four passengers as yet in that convenience. Before my comrade and I fell asleep, we
had some conversation about the good humor of
our landlord, which gave Strap such an idea of
his benevolence, that he positively believed we
should pay nothing for our lodging and entertainment. "Don't you observe," said he, "that he
has conceived a particular affection for us; nay,
even treated us at supper with extraordinary
fare, which, to be sure, we should not of ourselves
have called for?"

I was partly of Strap's opinion; but the experience I had of the world made me suspend my
belief till the morning, when, getting up betimes,
we breakfasted with our host and his daughter
on hasty-pudding and ale, and desired to know
what we had to pay. "Biddy will let you know,
gentlemen," said he, "for I never mind these matters. Money matters are beneath the concern of
one who lives upon the Horatian plan. *Crescen-
tem sequitur cura pecuniam.*" Meanwhile, Biddy
having consulted a slate that hung in the corner,
told us our reckoning came to 8s. 7d. "Eight
shillings and sevenpence!" cried Strap; "'tis impossible—you must be mistaken, young woman."
"Reckon again, child," says her father, very de-
liberately; "perhaps you have miscounted."

"No, indeed, father," she replied, "I know my business better." I could contain my indignation no longer, but said it was an unconscionable bill, and demanded to know the particulars; upon which the old man got up, muttering, "Ay, ay, let us see the particulars—that's but reasonable." And, taking pen, ink, and paper, wrote the following items:—

	s.	d.
To bread and beer	0	6
To a fowl and sausages	2	6
To four bottles *quadrim*	2	0
To fire and tobacco	0	7
To lodging	2	0
To breakfast	1	0
	8	7

As he had not the appearance of a common publican, and had raised a sort of veneration in me by his demeanor the preceding night, it was not in my power to upbraid him as he deserved; therefore I contented myself with saying, I was sure he did not learn to be an extortioner from Horace. He answered, I was but a young man, and did not know the world, or I would not tax him with extortion, whose only aim was to live *"contentus parvo,* and keep off *importuna pauperies."* My fellow-traveler could not so easily put up with this imposition; but swore he should either take one-third of the money, or go without. While we were engaged in this dispute, I perceived the daughter go out, and conjecturing the occasion, immediately paid the exorbitant demand, which was no sooner done, than Biddy returned with two stout fellows, who came in on pretense of taking their morning draught; but in reality to frighten us into compliance. Just as we departed, Strap, who was half distracted on account of this piece of expense, went up to the schoolmaster, and grinning in his face, pronounced with great emphasis, *"Semper avarus eget."* To which the pedant replied, with a malicious smile, *"Animum rege, qui, nisi paret, imperat."*

CHAPTER ELEVEN

WE traveled half a mile without exchang-
ing one word; my thoughts being engrossed by the knavery of the world, to
which I must be daily exposed; and the contem-
plation of my finances, which began sensibly
to diminish. At length Strap, who could hold no
longer, addressed me thus: "Well, fools and
their money are soon parted. If my advice had
been taken, that old skinflint should have been
damn'd before he had got more than the third of
his demand.—'Tis a sure sign you came easily by
your money, when you squander it away in this
manner. Ah, God help you, how many bristly
beards must I have mowed before I earned four
shillings and threepence halfpenny, which is all
thrown to the dogs? How many days have I sat
weaving hair, till my toes were numbed by the
cold, my fingers cramp'd, and my nose as blue
as the sign of the periwig that hung over the
door? What the devil was you afraid of? I
would have engaged to box with any one of those
fellows that came in, for a guinea. I'm sure I
have beat stouter men than either of them." And
indeed my companion would have fought anybody,

when his life was in no danger; but he had a
mortal aversion to firearms, and all instruments
of death. In order to appease him, I assured
him, no part of this extraordinary expense should
fall upon his shoulders; at which declaration he
was affronted, and told me, he would have me to
know, that, although he was a poor barber's boy,
he had a soul to spend his money with the best
squire of the land. Having walked all day at a
great pace, without halting for a refreshment,
we descried, toward the evening, to our inexpressible joy, the wagon about a quarter of a mile before us; and by that time we reached it, were both
of us so weary, that I verily believe it would have
been impracticable for us to have walked one
mile farther. We therefore bargained with the
driver, whose name was Joey, to give us a cast
to the next stage for a shilling; at which place
we should meet the master of the wagon, with
whom we might agree for the rest of the journey.

Accordingly, the convenience stopped, and Joey
having placed the ladder, Strap (being loaded
with our baggage) mounted first; but, just as he
was getting in, a tremendous voice assailed his
ears in these words: "God's fury! there shall
no passengers come here." The poor shaver was
so disconcerted at this exclamation, which both
he and I imagined proceeded from the mouth of
a giant, that he descended with great velocity, and
a countenance as white as paper. Joey perceiving our astonishment, called with an arch sneer,
"Waunds, coptain, whay woan't you sooffer the
poor waggoneer to meake a penny? Coom, coom,

young man, get oop, get oop, never moind the coptain—I'se not afear'd of the coptain.'' This was
not encouragement sufficient to Strap, who could
not be prevailed upon to venture up again; upon
which I attempted, though not without a quaking
heart, when I heard the same voice muttering
like distant thunder, ''Hell and the devil con-
found me, if I don't make you smart for this!''
However, I crept in, and by accident, got an
empty place in the straw, which I immediately
took possession of, without being able to discern the faces of my fellow-travelers in the dark.
Strap following with the knapsack on his back,
chanced to take the other side, and, by a jolt of
the carriage, pitched directly upon the stomach
of the captain, who bellowed out in a most dreadful manner, ''Blood and thunder, where's my
sword?'' At these words, my frighted comrade
started up, and at one spring bounced against
me with such force, that I thought he was the
supposed son of Anak, who intended to press me
to death. In the meantime, a female voice cried,
''Bless me? what is the matter, my dear?'' ''The
matter,'' replied the captain, ''d—n my blood! my
guts are squeezed into a pancake by that Scotchman's hump.'' Strap, trembling all the while at
my back, asked him pardon, and laid the blame
of what had happened upon the jolting of the
wagon; and the woman who spoke before, went
on: ''Ay, ay, my dear, it is our own fault; we
may thank ourselves for all the inconveniences
we meet with. I thank God I never traveled so
before. I'm sure, if my lady or Sir John was to

know where we are, they would not sleep this night for vexation. I wish to God we had writ for the chariot: I know we shall never be forgiven."—"Come, come, my dear," replied the captain, "it don't signify fretting now—we shall laugh it over as a frolic—I hope you will not suffer in your health. I shall make my lord very merry with our adventures in the diligence."

This discourse gave me such a high notion of the captain and his lady, that I durst not venture to join in the conversation. But immediately after, another female voice began: "Some people give themselves a great many needless airs —better folks than any here have traveled in wagons before now. Some of us have rode in coaches and chariots, with three footmen behind them, without making so much fuss about it. What then? we are now all upon a footing; therefore let's be sociable and merry. What do you say, Isaac? Is not this a good motion, you doting rogue? Speak, you old cent. per cent. fornicator. What desperate debts are you thinking of? What mortgage are you planning? Well, Isaac, positively you shall never gain my favor till you turn over a new leaf, grow honest, and live like a gentleman. In the meantime, give me a kiss, you old fumbler." These words, accompanied with a hearty smack enlivened the person to whom they were addressed to such a degree, that he cried in a transport, though with a faltering voice, "Ah! you wanton baggage—upon my credit, you are a waggish girl, he, he, he." This laugh introduced a fit of coughing, which almost

suffocated the poor usurer (such, we afterward
found, was the profession of this our fellow-traveler). About this time I fell asleep, and enjoyed
a comfortable nap, till such time as we arrived at
the inn where we put up. Here, having alighted
from the wagon, I had an opportunity of viewing
the passengers in order as they entered. The
first who appeared was a brisk, airy girl, about
twenty years old, with a silver-laced hat on her
head, instead of a cap, a blue stuff riding-suit
trimmed with silver, very much tarnished, and a
whip in her hand. After her came limping an
old man, with a worsted night-cap, buttoned under
his chin, and a broad-brimmed hat slouched over
it, an old rusty blue cloak tied about his neck,
under which appeared a brown surtout, that covered a threadbare coat and waistcoat, and, as we
afterward discerned, a dirty flannel jacket. His
eyes were hollow, bleared, and gummy; his face
was shriveled into a thousand wrinkles, his gums
were destitute of teeth, his nose sharp and droop-
ing, his chin peaked and prominent, so that, when
he mumped or spoke, they approached one another like a pair of nut-crackers; he supported
himself on an ivory-headed cane; and his whole
figure was a just emblem of winter, famine, and
avarice. But how was I surprised, when I beheld the formidable captain in the shape of a little thin creature, about the age of forty, with a
long withered visage, very much resembling that
of a baboon, through the upper part of which two
little gray eyes peeped: he wore his own hair
in a queue that reached to his rump, which im-

moderate length, I suppose, was the occasion of
a baldness that appeared on the crown of his head,
when he deigned to take off his hat, which was
very much of the size and cock of Pistol's.

Having laid aside his great-coat, I could not
help admiring the extraordinary make of this
man of war: he was about five feet and three
inches high, sixteen inches of which went to his
face and long scraggy neck; his thighs were about
six inches in length, his legs resembling spindles
or drumsticks, two feet and a half, and his body,
which put me in mind of extension without sub-
stance, engrossed the remainder; so that, on the
whole, he appeared like a spider or grasshopper
erect, and was almost a *vox et præterea nihil.*
His dress consisted of a frock of what is called
bear-skin, the skirts of which were about half
a foot long, an hussar waistcoat, scarlet breeches,
reaching halfway down his thighs, worsted stockings, rolled up almost to his groin, and shoes with
wooden heels at least two inches high: he carried
a sword very near as long as himself in one hand,
and with the other conducted his lady, who
seemed to be a woman of his own age, and still
retained some remains of an agreeable person;
but so ridiculously affected, that, had I not been a
novice in the world, I might have easily perceived
in her the deplorable vanity and second-hand airs
of a lady's woman. We were all assembled in the
kitchen, when Captain Weazel (for that was his
name) desired a room with a fire for himself and
spouse, and told the landlord they would sup by
themselves. The inn-keeper replied, that he could

not afford them a room by themselves; and as for
supping, he had prepared victuals for the passengers in the wagon, without respect of persons;
but if he could prevail on the rest to let him have
his choice in a separate manner, he should be very
well pleased. This was no sooner said, than all
of us declared against the proposal; and Miss
Jenny, our other female passenger, observed,
that, if Captain Weazel and his lady had a mind
to sup by themselves, they might wait until we
should have done. At this hint, the captain put
on a martial frown, and looked very big, without
speaking; while his yoke-fellow, with a disdainful
toss of her nose, muttered something about
"Creature!" which Miss Jenny overhearing,
stepped up to her, saying, "None of your names,
good Mrs. Abigail. Creature, quotha—I'll assure you, no such creature as you, neither—no
ten pound sneaker—no quality coupler."—Here
the captain interposed, with a "D—me, madam,
what do you mean by that?"—"D—n you, sir,
who are you?" replied Miss Jenny, "who made
you a captain, you pitiful, trencher-scraping,
pimping curler?—'Sdeath! the army is come to a
fine pass, when such fellows as you get commis-
sions—what, I suppose you think I don't know
you?—Egad, you and your helpmate are well met
—a cast-off mistress and a bald valet-de-chambre
are well yoked together." "Blood and wounds!"
cried Weazel, "d'ye question the honor of my
wife, madam!—Hell and d—tion! No man in
England durst say so much. I would flea him—
carbonado him! Fury and destruction! I would

have his liver for my supper.'' So saying, he drew his sword, and flourished with it, to the great terror of Strap; while Miss Jenny, snapping her fingers, told him, she did not value his resentment a louse. In the midst of this quarrel, the master of the wagon alighted, who understanding the cause of the disturbance, and fearing the captain and his lady would take umbrage, and leave his carriage, was at great pains to have everything made up, which he at last accomplished, and we sat down to supper all together. At bedtime we were shown to our apartments: the old usurer, Strap, and I, to one room; the captain, his wife, and Miss Jenny, to another. About midnight, my companion's bowels being disordered, he got up, in order to go backward; but, in his return, mistaking one door for another, entered Weazel's chamber, and without any hesitation, went to bed to his wife, who was fast asleep; the captain being at another end of the room, groping for some empty vessel, in lieu of his own chamber-pot, which was leaky: as he did not perceive Strap coming in, he went toward his own bed, after having found a convenience; but no sooner did he feel a rough head, covered with a cotton night-cap, than it came into his mind, that he had mistaken Miss Jenny's bed instead of his own, and that the head he felt was that of some gallant, with whom she had made an assignation. Full of this conjecture, and scandalized at the prostitution of his apartment, he snatched up the vessel he had just before filled, and emptied it at once on the astonished barber and his own wife,

who waking at that instant, broke forth into lamentable cries, which not only alarmed the husband beyond measure, but frightened poor Strap
almost out of his senses; for he verily believed
himself bewitched; especially when the incensed
captain seized him by the throat, with a volley
of oaths, asking him how he durst have the presumption to attempt the chastity of his wife.
Poor Strap was so amazed and confounded, that
he could say nothing, but, "I take God to witness,
she a virgin for me." Mrs. Weazel enraged to
find herself in such a pickle, through the precipitation of her husband, arose in her shift, and
with the heel of her shoe, which she found by
the bedside, belabored the captain's bald pate,
till he roared, "Murder." "I'll teach you to
empty your stink-pots on me," cried she, "you
pitiful hop-my-thumb coxcomb. What! I warrant you're jealous, you man of lath. Was it for
this I condescended to take you to my bed, you
poor withered sapless twig?" The noise occasioned by this adventure had brought the master
of the wagon and me to the door, where we overheard all that passed with great satisfaction. In
the meantime. we were alarmed with the cry of
"Rape! murder! rape!" which Miss Jenny pronounced with great vociferation.—"O! you vile
abominable old villain," said she, "would you rob
me of my virtue? But I'll be revenged of you,
you old goat! Help!—Help! for heaven's sake!
help!—I shall be ravished—ruined! help!" Some
servants of the inn hearing the cry, came running upstairs with lights, and such

chance afforded, when we beheld a very diverting
scene. In one corner stood the poor captain,
shivering in his shirt, which was all torn to rags,
with a woeful visage, scratched all over by his
wife, who had by this time wrapped the counter-
pane about her, and sat sobbing on the side of
her bed. In the other end lay the old usurer,
sprawling on Miss Jenny's bed, with his flannel
jacket over his shirt, and his tawny meager limbs
exposed to the air; while she held him fast by
the two ears, and loaded him with execrations.
When we asked what was the matter, she affected to weep; told us, she was afraid that wicked
rogue had ruined her in her sleep; and bade us
take notice of what we saw, for she intended to
make use of our evidence against him. The poor
wretch looked like one more dead than alive, and
begged to be released; a favor which he had no
sooner obtained, than he protested she was no
woman, but a devil incarnate; that she had first
seduced his flesh to rebel, and then betrayed him.
"Yes, cockatrice," continued he, "you know you
laid this snare for me, but you shan't succeed,
for I will hang myself before you shall get a
farthing off me." So saying, he crawled to his
own bed, groaning all the way. We then advanced to the captain, who told us, "Gentlemen,
here has been a d—ned mistake; but I'll be revenged on him who was the occasion of it. That
Scotchman who carries the knapsack shall not
breathe this vital air another day, if my name be
Weazel. My dear, I ask you ten thousand par-
dons; you are sensible I could mean no harm

to you."—"I know not what you meant," replied she, sighing, "but I know I have got enough to send me to my grave." At length they were reconciled. The wife was complimented with a share of Miss Jenny's bed (her own being overflowed), and the master of the wagon invited Weazel to sleep the remaining part of the night with him. I retired to mine, where I found Strap mortally afraid, he having stole away in the dark, while the captain and his lady were at loggerheads.

CHAPTER TWELVE

Captain Weazel challenges Strap, who declines the Combat
—An Affair between the Captain and me—The Usurer
is fain to give Miss Jenny five Guineas for a Release—
We are in danger of losing a Meal—The Behavior of
Weazel, Jenny, and Joey, on that occasion—An Account
of Captain Weazel and his Lady—The Captain's Courage
tried—Isaac's Mirth at the Captain's expense.

NEXT morning I agreed to give the master
of the wagon ten shillings for my passage to London, provided Strap should be
allowed to take my place when I should be dis-
posed to walk—at the same time I desired him to
appease the incensed captain, who had entered the
kitchen with a drawn sword in his hand, and
threatened, with many oaths, to sacrifice the villain who attempted to violate his bed; but it was
to no purpose for the master to explain the mistake, and assure him of the poor lad's innocence,
who stood trembling behind me all the while. The
more submission that appeared in Strap, the more
implacable seemed the resentment of Weazel, who
swore he must either fight him, or he would instantly put him to death. I was extremely provoked at this insolence, and told him, it could not
be supposed that a poor barber lad would engage
a man of the sword at his own weapon; but I was
persuaded he would wrestle or box with him. To
which proposal Strap immediately gave assent,

by saying, he would box with him for a guinea.
Weazel replied, with a look of disdain, that it
was beneath any gentleman of his character to
fight like a porter, or even to put himself on a
footing, in any respect, with such a fellow as
Strap. "Odds bodikins!" cries Joey, "sure, coptain, yaw would not commit moorder! Here's a
poor lad that is willing to make atoonement for
his offense; and an that woan't satisfie yaw, offers to fight yaw fairly. An yaw woan't box, I
dare say, he will coodgel with yaw,—woan't yaw,
my lad?"—Strap, after some hesitation, answered, "Yes, yes, I'll cudgel with him." But
this expedient being also rejected by the captain, I began to smell his character, and, tipping
Strap the wink, told the company that I had always heard it said, the person who receives a
challenge should have the choice of the weapons;
this therefore being the rule in point of honor,
I would venture to promise, on the head of my
companion, that he would even fight Captain
Weazel at sharps, but it should be with such
sharps as Strap was best acquainted with,
namely, razors. At my mentioning razors, I
could perceive the captain's color change, while
Strap, pulling me by the sleeve, whispered with
great eagerness, "No, no, no; for the love of God,
don't make any such bargain." At length Weazel recovering himself, returned toward me, and,
with a ferocious countenance, asked, "Who the
devil are you? will you fight me?" With these
words, putting himself in a posture, I was grievously alarmed at seeing the point of a sword

within half a foot of my breast; and, springing
to one side, snatched up a spit that stood in the
chimney-corner, with which I kept my formidable
adversary at bay, who made a great many half-
lunges, skipping backward at every push, till at
last I pinned him up in a corner, to the no small
diversion of the company.

While he was in this situation, his wife entered,
and, seeing her husband in these dangerous circumstances, uttered a dreadful scream: in this
emergency, Weazel demanded a cessation, which
was immediately granted; and at last was contented with the submission of Strap, who, falling
upon his knees before him, protested the innocence of his intention, and asked pardon for the
mistake he had committed. This affair being
ended without bloodshed, we went to breakfast,
but missed two of our company, namely, Miss
Jenny and the usurer. As for the first, Mrs.
Weazel informed us, that she had kept her awake
all night with her groans; and that, when she rose
in the morning, Miss Jenny was so much indis-
posed, that she could not proceed on her journey.
At that instant, a message came from her to the
master of the wagon, who immediately went into
her chamber, followed by us all. She told him in
a lamentable tone, that she was afraid of a mis-
carriage, owing to the fright she received last
night from the brutality of Isaac; and, as the
event was uncertain, desired the usurer might be
detained to answer for the consequence. Accordingly, this ancient Tarquin was found in the
wagon, whither he had retired to avoid the shame

of last night's disgrace, and brought by force into
her presence. He no sooner appeared, than she
began to weep and sigh most piteously, and told
us, if she died, she would leave her blood upon
the head of that ravisher. Poor Isaac turned up
his eyes and hands to heaven, prayed that God
would deliver him from the machinations of that
Jezebel; and assured us, with tears in his eyes,
that his being found in bed with her was the result
of her own invitation. The wagoner understanding the case, advised Isaac to make it up, by giving her a sum of money; to which advice he replied, with great vehemence, "A sum of money!
—a halter for the cockatrice!"—"Oh! 'tis very
well," said Miss Jenny: "I see it is in vain to attempt that flinty heart of his by fair means.
Joey, be so good as to go to the justice, and tell
him there is a sick person here, who wants to see
him on an affair of consequence." At the name
of justice, Isaac trembled, and, bidding Joey stay,
asked with a quivering voice, what she would
have? She told him, that as he had not perpe-
trated his wicked purpose, she would be satisfied
with a small matter. And though the damage she
might sustain in her health might be irreparable,
she would give him a release for an hundred
guineas. "An hundred guineas;" cried he, in an
ecstasy, "an hundred furies! Where should a
poor old wretch like me have an hundred guineas?
If I had so much money, d'ye think I should be
found traveling in a wagon at this season of the
year?" "Come, come," replied Jenny, "none of
your miserly artifice here. You think I don't

know Isaac Rapine, the money-broker, in the Min-
ories. Ah! you old rogue! many a pawn have
you had of me and my acquaintance, which was
never redeemed.'' Isaac finding it was in vain to
disguise himself, offered twenty shillings for a
discharge, which she absolutely refused under
fifty pounds. At last, however, she was brought
down to five, which he paid, with great reluctancy,
rather than be prosecuted for a rape. After
which accommodation the sick person made shift
to get into the wagon, and we set forward in great
tranquillity, Strap being accommodated with
Joey's horse, the driver himself choosing to walk.

This morning and forenoon we were entertained
with an account of the valor of Captain Weazel,
who told us he had once knocked down a soldier
that made game of him; tweaked a drawer by the
nose, who found fault with his picking his teeth
with a fork, at another time; and that he had
moreover challenged a cheesemonger, who had
the presumption to be his rival;—for the truth of
which exploits he appealed to his wife. She confirmed whatever he said, and observed, ''The last
affair happened that very day on which I received a love-letter from Squire Gobble; and don't
you remember, my dear, I was prodigiously sick
that very night with eating ortolans, when my
Lord Diddle took notice of my complexion's being altered, and my lady was so alarmed that she
had well-nigh fainted.'' ''Yes, my dear,'' replied
the captain, ''you know, my lord said to me, with
a sneer, 'Billy, Mrs. Weazel is certainly breed-
ing.' And I answered cavalierly, 'My lord, I

wish I could return the compliment.' Upon
which the whole company broke out into an immoderate fit of laughter; and my lord, who loves
a repartee dearly, came round and bussed me.''

We traveled in this manner five days, without
interruption, or meeting anything worth notice:
Miss Jenny, who soon recovered her spirits, entertaining us every day with diverting songs,
of which she could sing a great number; and rally-
ing her old gallant, who, notwithstanding, would
never be reconciled to her. On the sixth day,
while we were about to sit down to dinner, the
innkeeper came and told us, that three gentlemen,
just arrived, had ordered the victuals to be carried to their apartment, although he had informed
them that they were bespoke by the passengers in
the wagon. To which information they had replied, ''The passengers in the wagon might be
d—ned,—their betters must be served before them
—they supposed it would be no hardship on such
travelers to dine upon bread and cheese for one
day.'' This was a terrible disappointment to us
all; and we laid our heads together how to remedy
it; when Miss Jenny observed, that Captain Weazel, being by profession a soldier, ought in this
case to protect and prevent us from being insulted. But the captain excused himself, saying,
he would not for all the world be known to have
traveled in a wagon; swearing at the same time,
that, could he appear with honor, they should eat
his sword sooner than his provision. Upon this
declaration, Miss Jenny, snatching his weapon,
drew it, and ran immediately into the kitchen,

I—7

where she threatened to put the cook to death if
he did not send the victuals into our chamber
immediately. The noise she made brought the
three strangers down, one of whom no sooner
perceived her, than he cried, "Ha! Jenny
Ramper! what the devil brought thee hither?"
"My dear Jack Rattle!" replied she, running
into his arms, "is it you? Then Weazel may go
to hell for a dinner—I shall dine with you."

They consented to this proposal with a great
deal of joy; and we were on the point of being
reduced to a very uncomfortable meal, when
Joey, understanding the whole affair, entered the
kitchen with a pitchfork in his hand, and swore
he would be the death of any man who should
pretend to seize the victuals prepared for the
wagon. This menace had like to have produced
fatal consequences; the three strangers drawing
their swords, and being joined by their servants,
and we ranging ourselves to the side of Joey;
when the landlord interposing, offered to part
with his own dinner to keep the peace, which was
accepted by the strangers; and we sat down at
table without any further molestation. In the
afternoon, I chose to walk along with Joey, and
Strap took my place. Having entered into a
conversation with this driver, I soon found him
to be a merry, facetious, good-natured fellow,
and withal very arch. He informed me, that
Miss Jenny was a common girl upon the town;
who falling into company with a recruiting
officer, he carried her down in the stage-coach
from London to Newcastle, where he had been

arrested for debt, and was now in prison; upon
which she was fain to return to her former way
of life, by this conveyance. He told me likewise,
that one of the gentleman's servants whom we
left at the inn, having accidentally seen Weazel,
immediately knew him, and acquainted Joey with
some particulars of his character. That he had
served my Lord Frizzle in quality of valet-de-
chambre many years, while he lived separate from
his lady: but, upon their reconciliation, she ex-
pressly insisted upon Weazel's being turned off,
as well as the woman he kept; when his lordship,
to get rid of them both with a good grace, proposed that he should marry his mistress, and he
would procure a commission for him in the army.
This expedient was agreed to; and Weazel is
now, by his lordship's interest, ensign in ——'s
regiment. I found he and I had the same sentiments with regard to Weazel's courage, which
we resolved to put to the trial, by alarming the
passengers with the cry of "A highwayman!"
as soon as an horseman should appear. This
scheme we put in practice towards the dusk, when
we descried a man on horseback approaching
us. Joey had no sooner intimated to the people
in the wagon, that he was afraid we should all
be robbed, than a general consternation arose.
Strap jumped out of the wagon, and hid himself
behind a hedge. The usurer put forth ejaculations, and made a rustling among the straw, which
made us conjecture he had hid something under
it. Mrs. Weazel, wringing her hands, uttered
lamentable cries; and the captain, to our great

amazement, began to snore; but this artifice did
not succeed; for Miss Jenny, shaking him by the
shoulder, bawled out, " 'Sdeath! captain, is this
a time to snore, when we are going to be robbed?
Get up, for shame, and behave like a soldier and
a man of honor." Weazel pretended to be in
a great passion for being disturbed, and swore
he would have his nap out if all the highwaymen
in England surrounded him. "D—n my blood!
what are you afraid of?" continued he, at the
same time trembling with such agitation, that the
whole carriage shook. This singular piece of behavior incensed Miss Ramper so much, that she
cried, "D—n our pitiful soul, you are as arrant
a poltroon as ever was drummed out of a regiment.—Stop the wagon, Joey—let me get out,
and by G—d, if I have rhetoric enough, the thief
shall not only take your purse, but your skin
also."

So saying, she leapt out with great agility.
By this time the horseman came up with us, and
happened to be a gentleman's servant well known
to Joey, who communicated the scheme, and desired him to carry it on a little further, by going
up to the wagon, and questioning those within.
The stranger consenting for the sake of diversion, approached it, and in a terrible tone, demanded, "Who have we got here?" Isaac replied, with a lamentable voice, "Here's a poor
miserable sinner, who has got a small family to
maintain, and nothing in the world wherewithal,
but these fifteen shillings, which if you rob me
of, we must all starve together." "Who's that

sobbing in the other corner?" said the supposed
highwayman. "A poor unfortunate woman,"
answered Mrs. Weazel, "upon whom I beg you
for Christ's sake to have compassion." "Are
you maid or wife?" said he. "Wife, to my
sorrow," cried she. "Who or where is your
husband?" continued he. "My husband," replied Mrs. Weazel, "is an officer in the army, and
was left sick at the last inn where we dined."
"You must be mistaken, madam," said he,
"for I myself saw him get into the wagon this
afternoon.—But pray what smell is that? Sure
your lap-dog has befouled himself;—let me catch
hold of the nasty cur, I'll teach him better
manners." Here he laid hold of one of Weazel's
legs and pulled him out from under his wife's pet-
ticoats, where he had concealed himself. The poor
trembling captain being detected in this inglorious
situation, rubbed his eyes, and affecting to wake
out of sleep, cried, "What's the matter?—what's
the matter?" "The matter is not much," answered the horseman, "I only called in to inquire
after your health, and so adieu, most noble captain." So saying, he clapt spurs to his horse,
and was out of sight in a moment. It was some
time before Weazel could recollect himself, but
at length re-assuming the big look he said,
"D—n the fellow! why did he ride away, before
I had time to ask him how his lord and lady do?—
Don't you remember Tom, my dear?" addressing himself to his wife. "Yes," replied she, "I
think I do remember something of the fellow—
but you know I seldom converse with people of

his station." "Hey-day," cried Joey, "do yaw
knaw the young mon, coptain?" "Know him,"
said Weazel, "many a time has he filled a glass
of Burgundy for me at my Lord Trippet's
table." "And what may his neame be, coptain?" said Joey. "His name?—his name," replied Weazel, "is Tim Rinser." "Waunds!"
cried Joey, "a has changed his own neame then!
for I'se lay a wager he was christened John
Trotter." This observation raised a laugh
against the captain, who seemed very much disconcerted; when Isaac broke silence, and said,
"It was no matter who or what he was, since he
has not proved the robber we suspected. And
we ought to bless God for our narrow escape."
"Bless God," said Weazel, "bless the devil! for
what? had he been a highwayman, I should have
eat his blood, body, and guts, before he had
robbed me, or any one in this *diligence.*" "Ha,
ha, ha;" cried Miss Jenny, "I believe you will
eat all you kill indeed, captain." The usurer
was so well pleased at the event of this adventure,
that he could not refrain from being severe, and
took notice, that Captain Weazel seemed to be a
good Christian, for he had armed himself with
patience and resignation, instead of carnal
weapons, and worked out his salvation with fear
and trembling. This piece of satire occasioned
a great deal of mirth at Weazel's expense, who
muttered a great many oaths, and threatened to
cut Isaac's throat. The usurer taking hold of this
menace, said, "Gentlemen and ladies, I take you
all to witness, that my life is in danger from this

bloody-minded officer. I'll have him bound over to the peace.'' This second sneer procured another laugh against him, and he remained crestfallen during the remaining part our journey.

CHAPTER THIRTEEN

WE arrived at our inn, supped, and went to bed; but Strap's distemper continuing, he was obliged to rise in the middle of the night, and taking the candle in his hand, which he had left burning for the purpose, he went down to the house of office, whence, in a short time, he returned in a great hurry, with his hair standing on end, and a look betokening horror and astonishment! Without speaking a word, he set down the light, and jumped into bed behind me, where he lay and trembled with great violence. When I asked him what was the matter? he replied, with a broken accent, "God have mercy on us!—I have seen the devil!" Though my prejudice was not quite so strong as his, I was not a little alarmed at this exclamation; and much more so, when I heard the sound of bells approaching our chamber, and felt my bedfellow cling close to me, uttering these words, "Christ have mercy upon us!—there he comes!"

At that instant, a monstrous overgrown raven entered our chamber, with bells at his feet, and made directly towards our bed. As this creature is reckoned in our country a common vehicle for the devil and witches to play their pranks in, I verily believed we were haunted, and, in a violent fright, shrunk under the bedclothes. This terrible apparition leapt upon the bed, and, after giving us several severe dabs with its beak through the blankets, hopped away and vanished. Strap and I recommended ourselves to the protection of Heaven with great devotion; and, when we no longer heard the noise, ventured to peep up and take breath. But we had not been long freed from this phantom, when another appeared, that had well-nigh deprived us both of our senses. We perceived an old man enter the room, with a long white beard that reached to his middle; there was a certain wild peculiarity in his eyes and countenance that did not savor of this world; and his dress consisted of a brown stuff coat, buttoned behind and at the wrists, with an odd-fashioned cap of the same stuff upon his head. I was so amazed, that I had not power to move my eyes from such a ghastly object, but lay motionless, and saw him come straight up to me. When he reached the bed, he wrung his hands, and cried, with a voice that did not seem to belong to a human creature, "Where is Ralph?" I made no reply; upon which he repeated, in an accent still more preternatural, "Where is Ralpho?" He had no sooner pronounced these words, than I heard the sound of

the bells at a distance; which the apparition having listened to, tripped away, and left me almost
petrified with fear. It was a good while before
I could recover myself so far as to speak; and
when at length I turned to Strap, I found him in
a fit, which, however, did not last long. When
he came to himself, I asked his opinion of what
had happened; and he assured me, that the first
must certainly be the soul of some person
damned, which appeared by the chains about his
legs, (for his fears had magnified the creature
to the bigness of a horse, and the sound of small
morrice-bells to the clanking of massy chains.)
As for the old man, he took it to be the spirit of
somebody murdered long ago in this place, which
had power granted to it to torment the assassin
in the shape of a raven, and that Ralpho was the
name of the said murderer. Although I had not
much faith in this interpretation, I was too much
troubled to enjoy any sleep, and in all my future
adventures never passed a night so ill. In the
morning, Strap imparted the whole affair to Joey,
who, after an immoderate fit of laughter, ex-
plained the matter, by telling him the old man
was the landlord's father, who had been an idiot
some years, and diverted himself with a tame
raven, which, it seems, had hopped away from
his apartment in the night, and induced him to
follow it to our chamber, where he had inquired
after it, under the name of Ralpho.

Nothing remarkable happened during the remaining part of our journey, which continued six
or seven days longer. At length, we entered the

great city, and lodged all night at the inn where
the wagon put up. Next morning, all the passengers parted different ways; while my companions and I sallied out to inquire for the member of parliament, to whom I had a letter of
recommendation from Mr. Crab. As we had discharged our lodging at the inn, Strap took up our
baggage and marched behind me in the street,
with the knapsack on his back, as usual, so that
we made a very whimsical appearance. I had
dressed myself to the greatest advantage—that
is, put on a clean ruffled shirt, and my best thread
stockings. My hair, which was of the deepest
red, hung down upon my shoulders, as lank and
straight as a pound of candles; and the skirts of
my coat reached to the middle of my leg; my
waistcoat and breeches were of the same piece,
and cut in the same taste; and my hat very much
resembled a barber's bason, in the shallowness of
the crown, and narrowness of the brim. Strap
was habited in a much less awkward manner; but
a short crop-eared wig that very much resembled
Scrub's in the play, and the knapsack on his back,
added to what is called a queer phiz, occasioned
by a long chin, hook nose, and high cheek-bones,
rendered him on the whole a very fit subject of
mirth and pleasantry.

As we walked along, Strap, at my desire, inquired of a carman, whom we met, whereabouts
Mr. Cringer lived; and was answered by a stare,
accompanied with the word, "Anan!" Upon
which I came up in order to explain the question,
but had the misfortune to be unintelligible like-

wise, the carman damning us for a lousy Scotch guard, and whipping his horses, with a "Gee ho!" which nettled me to the quick, and roused the indignation of Strap so far, that, after the fellow was gone a good way, he told me he would fight him for a farthing. While we were deliberating upon what was to be done, an hackney coachman driving softly along, and perceiving us standing by the kennel, came up close to us, and calling, "A coach, master!" by a dexterous management of the reins, made his horses stumble in the wet, and bedaub us all over with mud. After which exploit, he drove on, applauding himself with a hearty laugh, in which several people joined, to my great mortification; but one, more compassionate than the rest, seeing us strangers, advised me to go into an alehouse and dry myself. I thanked him for his advice, which I immediately complied with; and going into the house he pointed out, called for a pot of beer, and sat down by a fire in the public room, where we cleaned ourselves as well as we could. In the meantime, a wag, who sat in a box, smoking his pipe, understanding by our dialect that we were from Scotland, came up to me, and, with a grave countenance, asked how long I had been caught? As I did not know the meaning of this question, I made no answer; and he went on, saying, it could not be a great while, for my tail was not yet cut; at the same time, taking hold of my hair, and tipping the wink to the rest of the company, who seemed highly entertained with his wit. I was incensed at this usage, but afraid of resenting it, because I happened to be in a strange place, and perceived the person who spoke to me was a brawny fellow, for whom I thought myself by no means a match. However, Strap having either more courage, or less caution, could not put up with the insults that I suffered; but told him, in a peremptory tone, "He was an uncivil fellow for making so free with his betters." Then the wit, going towards him, asked him what he had got in his knapsack? "Is it oatmeal, or brimstone, Sawney?" said he, seizing him by the chin, which he shook, to the inexpressible diversion of all present. My companion, feeling himself assaulted in such an opprobrious manner disengaged himself in a trice, and lent his antagonist such a box on the ear, as made him stagger to the other side of the room; and, in a moment, a ring was formed for the combatants. Seeing Strap beginning to strip, and my blood being heated with indignation, which banished all other thoughts, I undressed myself to the skin in an instant, and declared, that as the affront that occasioned the quarrel was offered to me, I would fight it out myself; upon which one or two cried out, "That's a brave Scotch boy; you shall have fair play, by G—d."

This assurance gave me fresh spirits, and going up to my adversary, who, by his pale countenance, did not seem much inclined to the battle, I struck him so hard on the stomach, that he reeled over the bench, and fell to the ground. Then I attempted to keep him down, in order to improve my success, according to the manner of my own country, but was restrained by the spectators, one of whom endeavored to raise up my opponent, but in vain; for he protested he would not fight, for he was not quite recovered of a late illness. I was very well pleased with this excuse, and immediately dressed myself having acquired the good opinion of the company for my bravery, as well as of my comrade Strap, who shook me by the hand, and wished me joy of the victory. After having drunk our pot, and dried our clothes, we inquired of the landlord if he knew Mr. Cringer, the member of parliament, and were amazed at his replying in the negative; for we imagined, he must be altogether as conspicuous here, as in the borough he represented; but he told us we might possibly hear of him as we passed along. We betook ourselves, therefore, to the street, where, seeing a footman standing at a door, we made up to him, and asked if he knew where our patron lived? This member of the party-colored fraternity, surveying us both very minutely, said he knew Mr. Cringer very well, and bade us turn down the first street on our left, then turn to the right, and then to the left again, after which perambulation we would observe a lane, through which we must pass, and at the other end we should find an alley that leads to another street, where we should see the sign of the Thistle and Three Pedlars, and there he lodged.

We thanked him for his information, and went forwards, Strap telling me, that he knew this person to be an honest friendly man, by his countenance, before he opened his mouth; in which opinion I acquiesced, ascribing his good manners to the company he daily saw in the house where he served. We followed his directions punctually, in turning to the left and to the right, and to the left again; but instead of seeing a lane before us, found ourselves at the side of the river, a circumstance that perplexed us not a little; and my fellow-traveler ventured to pronounce, that we had certainly missed our way. By this time we were pretty much fatigued with our walk, and not knowing how to proceed, I went into a small snuff shop hard by, encouraged by the sign of the Highlander, where I found, to my inexpressible satisfaction, the shopkeeper was my countryman. He was no sooner informed of our peregrination, and the direction we had received from the footman, than he informed us, we had been imposed upon, telling us, Mr. Cringer lived in the other end of the town; and that it would be to no purpose for us to go thither to-day, for by that time he was gone to the House. I then asked if he could recommend us to a lodging. He readily gave us a line to one of his acquaintance, who kept a chandler's shop not far from St. Martin's Lane; there we hired a bedroom, up two pair of stairs, at the rate of 2s. per week, so very small, that, when the bed was let down, we were obliged to carry out every other piece of furniture that belonged to the apartment, and use the bedstead by way of chairs. About dinnertime, our landlord asked us how we proposed to live? to which interrogation we answered, that we would be directed by him. "Well, then," says he, "there are two ways of eating in this town, for people of your condition—the one more creditable and expensive than the other; the first is, to dine at an eating-house, frequented by well-dressed people only; and the other is called diving, practiced by those who are either obliged or inclined to live frugally." I gave him to understand, that, provided the last was not infamous, it would suit much better with our circumstances than the other. "Infamous," cried he, "God forbid! there are many creditable people, rich people, ay, and fine people, that dive every day. I have seen many a pretty gentleman, with a laced waistcoat, dine in that manner very comfortable for threepence halfpenny, and go afterwards to the coffee-house, where he made a figure with the best lord in the land; but your own eyes shall bear witness—I will go along with you to-day, and introduce you." He accordingly conducted us to a certain lane, where stopping, he bade us observe him, and do as he did; and, walking a few paces, dived into a cellar, and disappeared in an instant.

I followed his example, and descending very successfully, found myself in the middle of a cook's shop, almost suffocated with the steams of boiled beef, and surrounded by a company of hackney coachmen, chairmen, draymen, and a few footmen out of place, or on board wages, who sat eating shin of beef, tripe, cowheel, or sausages, at separate boards, covered with cloths, which turned my stomach. While I stood in amaze, undetermined whether to sit down or walk up-

wards again, Strap, in his descent, missing one
of the steps, tumbled headlong into this infernal
ordinary, and overturned the cook, as she carried
a porringer soup to one of the guests. In her
fall, she dashed the whole mess against the legs
of a drummer, belonging to the foot-guards, who
happened to be in her way, and scalded him so
miserably, that he started up, and danced up and
down, uttering a volley of execrations, that made
my hair stand on end. While he entertained
the company in this manner, with an eloquence
peculiar to himself, the cook got up, and, after a
hearty curse on the poor author of this mis-
chance, who lay under the table, scratching his
rump with a woeful countenance, emptied a salt-
cellar in her hand, and stripping down the
patient's stocking, which brought the skin along
with it, applied the contents to the sore. This
poultice was scarce laid on, when the drummer,
who had begun to abate of his exclamation, broke
forth into such a hideous yell, as made the whole
company tremble; then, seizing a pewter pinto
pot that stood by him, squeezed the sides of it
together, as if it had been made of pliant leather,
grinding his teeth at the same time with a most
horrible grin. Guessing the cause of this violent
transport, I bade the woman wash off the salt,
and bathe the part with oil, which she did, and
procured him immediate ease. But here another
difficulty occurred, which was no other than the
landlady's insisting on his paying for the pot he
had rendered useless. He swore he would pay
for nothing but what he had eaten, and bade her

be thankful for this moderation, or else he would prosecute her for damages. Strap, foreseeing the whole affair would lie at his door, promised to satisfy the cook, and called for a dram of gin to treat the drummer, which entirely appeased him, and composed all animosities. After this accommodation, our landlord and we sat down at a board, and dined upon shin of beef most deliciously; our reckoning amounting to two-pence halfpenny each, bread and small beer included.

CHAPTER FOURTEEN

IN the afternoon my companion proposed to
call at his friend's house, which, we were
informed, was in the neighborhood;
whither we accordingly went, and were so lucky
as to find him at home. This gentleman, who had
come from Scotland three or four years before,
kept a school in town, where he taught the Latin,
French, and Italian languages; but what he
chiefly professed was the pronunciation of the
English tongue, after a method more speedy and
uncommon than any practiced heretofore; and,
indeed, if his scholars spoke like their master, the
latter part of his undertaking was certainly performed to a tittle; for although I could easily
understand every word of what I had heard
hitherto since I entered England, three parts in
four of his dialect were as unintelligible to me as
if he had spoken in Arabic or Irish. He was a
middle-sized man, and stooped very much, though
not above the age of forty; his face frightfully
pitted with the smallpox, and his mouth extended
from ear to ear. He was dressed in a night-

gown of plaid, fastened about his middle with a
sergeant's old sash, and a tie periwig, with a foretop three inches high, in the fashion of King
Charles the Second's reign. After he had received Strap (who was related to him) very
courteously, he inquired of him who I was, and,
being informed, took me by the hand, telling me
he was at school with my father. When he understood my situation, he assured me that he
would do me all the service in his power, both by
his advice and otherwise; and, while he spoke
these words, eyed me with great attention, walking round me several times, and muttering,
"O Ch—st! O Ch—st! fat a saight is here?" I
soon guessed the reason of his ejaculation, and
said, "I suppose, sir, you are not pleased with
my dress?" "Dress," answered he; "you may
caal it fat you please in your country, but I vaw
to Gad, 'tis a masquerade here. No Christian
will admit such a figure into his hawse. Upon
my conscience! I wonder the dogs did not hunt
you. Did you pass through St. James's market?
God bless my eye-saight! you look like a cousin-
german of Ouran Outang."—I began to be a little
serious at this discourse, and asked him if he
thought I should obtain entrance to-morrow at the
house of Mr. Cringer, on whom I chiefly depended
for an introduction into business. "Mr. Cringer,
Mr. Cringer," replied he, scratching his cheek,
"may be a very honest gentleman—I know nothing to the contrary; but is your sole dependence
upon him? Who recommended you to him?" I
pulled out Mr. Crab's letter, and told him the

foundation of my hopes; at which he started at
me, and repeated, "Ch—st!" I began to conceive bad omens from this behavior of his, and
begged he would assist me with his advice, which
he promised to give me frankly; and, as a speci-
men, directed us to a periwig warehouse in the
neighborhood, in order to be accommodated; laying strong injunctions on me not to appear before
Mr. Cringer till I had parted with these carroty
locks, which he said were sufficient to beget an
antipathy against me in all mankind. And, as
we were going to pursue this advice, he called me
back, and bade me be sure to deliver my letter
into Mr. Cringer's own hand. As we walked
along Strap triumphed greatly in our reception
with his friend, who, it seems, had assured him
he would, in a day or two, provide for him with
some good master; and "Now," says he, "you
shall see how I shall fit you with a wig. There's
ne'er a barber in London, and that's a bold word,
can palm a rotten caul, or a pennyweight of dead
hair upon me." And, indeed, this zealous ad-
herent did wrangle so long with the merchant
that he was desired twenty times to leave the
shop, and see if he could get one cheaper else-
where. At length I made choice of a good handsome bob, for which I paid ten shillings, and
returned to our lodging, where Strap in a moment rid me of that hair which had given the
schoolmaster so much offense.

We got up next day betimes, having been informed that Mr. Cringer gave audience by
candle-light to all his dependants, he himself

being obliged to attend the levee of my Lord
Terrier at break of day; because his lordship
made one at the minister's between eight and nine
o'clock. When we came to Mr. Cringer's door,
Strap, to give me an instance of his politeness,
ran to the knocker, which he employed so loud
and so long that he alarmed the whole street;
and a window opening in the second story of the
next house, a chamber-pot was discharged upon
him so successfully that the poor barber was wet
to the skin, while I, being luckily at some distance, escaped the unsavory deluge. In the
meantime a footman opening the door, and seeing nobody in the street, but us, asked with a
stern countenance if it was I who made such a
d—ned noise, and what I wanted? I told him
I had business with his master, whom I desired
to see. Upon which he clapped the door in my
face, telling me I must learn better manners
before I could have access to his master. Vexed
at this disappointment, I turned my resentment
against Strap, whom I sharply reprimanded for
his presumption; but he, not in the least regarding what I said, wrung the urine out of his
periwig, and lifting up a large stone, flung it
with such force against the street door of that
house from whence he had been bedewed, that the
lock giving way, it flew wide open, and he took
to his heels, leaving me to follow him as I could.
Indeed there was no time for deliberation; I
therefore pursued him with all the speed I could
exert, until we found ourselves about the dawn
in a street we did not know. Here, as we

wandered along gaping about, a very decent sort
of a man passing by me, stopped of a sudden,
and took up something, which having examined,
he turned and presented it to me with these
words: "Sir, you have dropped half a crown."
I was not a little surprised at this instance of
honesty, and told him it did not belong to me;
but he bade me recollect, and see if all my money
was safe: upon which I pulled out my purse (for
I had bought one since I came to town), and
reckoning my money in my hand, which was now
reduced to five guineas seven shillings and two-
pence, assured him I had lost nothing.

"Well, then," says he, "so much the better—
this is a godsend; and, as you two were present
when I picked it up, you are entitled to equal
shares with me." I was astonished at these
words, and looked upon this person to be a
prodigy of integrity, but absolutely refused to
take any part of the sum. "Come, gentlemen,"
said he, "you are too modest—I see you are
strangers; but you shall give me leave to treat
you with a whet this cold raw morning." I would
have declined this invitation, but Strap whispered
to me that the gentleman would be affronted, and
I complied. "Where shall we go?" said the
stranger, "I am quite ignorant of this part of the
town." I informed him that we were in the same
situation: upon which he proposed to go into the
first public-house we should find open; and, as we
walked together, he began in this manner: "I
find by your tongues you are from Scotland, gentlemen. My grandmother by the father's side

was of your country; and I am so prepossessed in
its favor that I never meet a Scotchman but my
heart warms. The Scots are a very brave people.
There is scarce a great family in the kingdom
that cannot boast of some exploits performed by
its ancestors many hundred years ago. There's
your Douglasses, Gordons, Campbells, Hamiltons.
We have no such ancient families here in England. Then you are all very well educated. I
have known a peddler talk in Greek and Hebrew,
as well as if they had been his mother tongue.
And, for honesty, I once had a servant, his name
was Gregory Macgregor: I would have trusted
him with untold gold.''—This eulogium on my native country gained my affection so strongly that
I believe I could have gone to death to serve the
author; and Strap's eyes swam in tears.

At length, as we passed through a dark narrow
lane, we perceived a public-house, which we entered, and found a man sitting by the fire smoking a pipe, with a pint of purl before him. Our
new acquaintance asked us if ever we had drank
egg-flip? To which question we answering in the
negative, he assured us of a regale, and ordered
a quart to be prepared, calling for pipes and tobacco at the same time. We found this composition very palatable, and drank heartily; the conversation, which was introduced by the gentleman, turning upon the snares that young unex-
perienced people are exposed to in this metrop-
olis. He described a thousand cheats that are
daily practiced upon the ignorant and unwary;
and warned us of them with so much good nature

and concern, that we blessed the opportunity
which threw us in his way. After we had put
the can about for some time, our new friend began to yawn, telling us he had been up all night
with a sick person; and proposed we should have
recourse to some diversion to keep him awake.
"Suppose," said he, "we should take a hand at
whist for pastime. But let me see, that won't do,
there's only three of us; and I cannot play at any
other game. The truth is, I seldom or never play,
but out of complaisance, or at such a time as this,
when I am in danger of falling asleep." Although I was not much inclined to gaming, I felt
no aversion to pass an hour or two at cards with
a friend; and knowing that Strap understood as
much of the matter as I, made no scruple of saying, "I wish we could find a fourth hand." While
we were in this perplexity, the person whom we
found in the house at our entrance overhearing
our discourse, took the pipe from his mouth very
gravely, and accosted us thus: "Gentlemen, my
pipe is out, you see (shaking the ashes into the
fire), and rather than you should be balked, I
don't care if I take a hand with you for a trifle;
but remember I won't play for anything of consequence." We accepted this proffer with pleasure.

Having cut for partners, it fell to my lot to play
with him against our friend and Strap, for threepence a game. We were so successful, that, in
a short time, I was half a crown gainer; when
the gentleman whom we had met in the street
observing he had no luck to-day, proposed to

leave off, or change partners. By this time I was inflamed with my good fortune and the expectation of improving it, as I perceived the two strangers played but indifferently. Therefore, I voted for giving him his revenge; and, cutting again, Strap and I, to our mutual satisfaction, happened to be partners. My good fortune attended me still; and in less than an hour we had got thirty shillings of their money; for, as they lost, they grew the keener, and doubled stakes every time. At last the inconstant goddess began to veer about; and we were very soon stripped of all our gains, and about forty shillings of our own money. This loss mortified me extremely, and had a visible effect on the muscles of Strap's face, which lengthened apace; but our antagonists perceiving our condition, kindly permitted us to retrieve our loss, and console ourselves with a new acquisition. Then my companion wisely suggested it was time to be gone; upon which the person who had joined us in the house began to curse the cards, and muttered that we were indebted to fortune only for what we had got, no part of our success being owing to our good play. This insinuation nettled me so much, that I challenged him to a game of piquet for a crown; and he was with difficulty persuaded to accept the invitation. This contest ended in less than an hour, to my inexpressible affliction, who lost every shilling of my own money, Strap absolutely refusing to supply me with a sixpence.

The gentleman at whose request we had come in, perceiving, by my disconsolate looks, the situation of my heart, which well-nigh bursted with grief and resentment, when the other stranger got up and went away with my money, began in this manner: "I am truly afflicted at your bad luck, and would willingly repair it, was it in my power. But what in the name of goodness could provoke you to tempt your fate so long? It is always a maxim with gamesters to pursue success as far as it will go, and to stop whenever fortune shifts about. You are a young man, and your passions too impetuous; you must learn to govern them better. However, there is no experience like that which is bought; you will be the better for this the longest day you have to live. As for the fellow who has got your money, I don't half like him. Did not you observe me tip you the wink to leave off in time?" I answered, "No." "No," continued he, "you was too eager to mind anything but the game. But harkee," said he, in a whisper, "are you satisfied of that young man's honesty? his looks are a little suspicious; but I may be mistaken; he made a great many grimaces while he stood behind you; this is a very wicked town." I told him I was very well convinced of my comrade's integrity, and that the grimaces he mentioned were doubtless owing to his anxiety at my loss. "Oho! if that be the case, I ask his pardon. Landlord, see what's to pay."—The reckoning amounted to eighteenpence, which having discharged, the gentleman shook us both by the hand, and, saying he should be very glad to see us again, departed.

CHAPTER FIFTEEN

IN our way to our lodging, after a profound
silence on both sides, Strap, with a hideous
groan, observed, that we had brought our
pigs to a fine market. To this observation I made
no reply; and he went on, "God send us well out
of this place; we have not been in London eight-
and-forty hours, and I believe we have met with
eight-and-forty thousand misfortunes.—We have
been jeered, reproached, buffeted, pissed upon,
and at last stripped of our money; and I suppose
by and by we shall be stripped of our skins.—Indeed, as to the money part of it, that was owing
to our own folly; Solomon says, *Bray a fool in a
mortar, and he will never be wise.* Ah! God help
us, an ounce of prudence is worth a pound of
gold." This was no time for him to tamper
with my disposition, already mad with my loss,
and inflamed with resentment against him for
having refused me a little money to attempt to

124

retrieve it. I therefore turned toward him with a stern countenance, and asked, who he called fool? Being altogether unaccustomed to such looks from me, he stood still, and stared in my face for some time; then, with some confusion, uttered, "Fool! I called nobody fool but myself; I am sure I am the greatest fool of the two, for being so much concerned at other people's misfortunes: but *nemo omnibus horis sapit* —that's all—that's all." Upon which a silence ensued, that brought us to our lodging, where I threw myself upon the bed in an agony of despair, resolved to perish rather than apply to my companion, or any other body, for relief; but Strap, who knew my temper, and whose heart bled within him at my distress, after some pause came to the bedside, and, putting a leather purse into my hand, burst into tears, crying, "I know what you think; but I scorn your thoughts. There's all I have in the world; take it, and I'll perhaps get more for you before that be done. If not, I'll beg for you, steal for you, go through the wide world with you, and starve with you; for though I be a poor cobbler's son, I am no scout." I was so touched with the generous passion of this poor creature, that I could not refrain from weeping also; and we mingled our tears together for some time. Upon examining the purse, I found in it two half guineas and half a crown, which I would have returned to him, saying, he knew better than I how to manage it; but he absolutely refused my proposal, and told me, it was more reasonable

and decent that he should depend upon me who
was a gentleman, than that I should be controlled
by him.

After this friendly contest was over, and our
minds more at ease, we informed our landlord of
what had happened to us, taking care to conceal
the extremity to which we were reduced. He no
sooner heard the story, than he assured us we
had been grievously imposed upon by a couple
of sharpers, who were associates; and that this
polite, honest, friendly, humane person, who had
treated us so civilly, was no other than a rascally money-dropper, who made it his business to
decoy strangers in that manner to one of his own
haunts, where an accomplice or two were always
waiting to assist in pillaging the prey he had run
down. Here the good man recounted a great
many stories of people who had been seduced,
cheated, pilfered, beat, nay even murdered by
such villains. I was confounded at the artifice
and wickedness of mankind; and Strap, lifting
up his eyes and hands to heaven, prayed that God
would deliver him from such scenes of iniquity;
for surely the devil had set up his throne in
London. Our landlord being curious to know
what reception we had met with at Mr. Cringer's,
we acquainted him with the particulars; at which
he shook his head, and told us, we had not gone
the right way to work; that there was nothing
to be done with a member of parliament without a
bribe; that the servant was commonly infected
with the master's disease, and expected to be paid
for his work, as well as his betters. He therefore

advised me to give the footman a shilling the next
time I should desire admittance to my patron, or
else I should scarce find an opportunity to deliver
my letter. Accordingly, next morning, when the
door was opened, I slipped a shilling into his
hand, and told him I had a letter for his master.
I found the good effects of my liberality; for the
fellow let me in immediately, and taking the letter out of my hand, desired me to wait in a kind
of passage for an answer. In this place I continued standing for three quarters of an hour,
during which time I saw a great many young
fellows, whom I formerly knew in Scotland, pass
and repass, with an air of familiarity, in their
way to and from the audience chamber; while I
was fain to stand shivering in the cold, and turn
my back to them, that they might not perceive
the lowness of my condition. At length Mr. Cringer came out to see a young gentleman to the
door, who was no other than Squire Gawky,
dressed in a very gay suit of clothes. At parting,
Mr. Cringer shook him by the hand, and told him
he hoped to have the pleasure of his company at
dinner; then turning about toward me, asked what
were my commands? When he understood I was
the person who had brought the letter from Mr.
Crab, he affected to recollect my name, which,
however, he pretended he could not do, till he had
consulted the letter again; to save him that trouble, I told him my name was Random. Upon
which he went on, "Ay, ay, Random, Random,
Random—I think I remember the name"; and
very well he might, for this very individual Mr.

Cringer had many a time rode before my grandfather's cloakbag in quality of a footman.
"Well," says he, "you propose to go on board
a man of war, as surgeon's mate." I replied by
a low bow. "I believe it will be a difficult matter," continued he, "to procure a warrant, there
being already such a swarm of Scotch surgeons
at the Navy Office, in expectation of the next vacancy, that the commissioners are afraid of being
torn to pieces, and have actually applied for a
guard to protect them. However, some ships will
soon be put in commission, and then we shall see
what's to be done." So saying, he left me ex-
ceedingly mortified at the different reception Mr.
Gawky and I had met with from this upstart,
proud, mean member, who, I imagined, would
have been glad of an opportunity to be grateful
for the obligations he owed to my family.

At my return, I was surprised with the agreeable news of Strap's being employed, on the recommendation of his friend the schoolmaster, by a
periwig-maker in the neighborhood, who allowed
him five shillings per week, besides bed and board.
I continued to dance attendance every other morning at the levee of Mr. Cringer, during a fortnight,
in which time I became acquainted with a young
fellow of my own country and profession, who
also depended on the member's interest; but was
treated with much more respect than I, both by
the servants and master, and often admitted into
a parlor, where there was a fire, for the convenience of the better sort of those who waited for
him. Thither I was never permitted to penetrate,

on account of my appearance, which was not at all fashionable: but was obliged to stand blowing my fingers in a cold lobby, and take the first opportunity of Mr. Cringer's going to the door to speak with him. One day, while I enjoyed this occasion, a person was introduced, whom Mr. Cringer no sooner saw, than, running toward him, he saluted him with a bow to the very ground, and afterward shaking him by the hand with great heartiness and familiarity, called him his good friend, and asked very kindly after Mrs. Staytape, and the young ladies; then, after a whisper which continued some minutes, wherein I overheard the word *honor* repeated several times with great emphasis, Mr. Cringer introduced me to this gentleman, as to a person whose advice and assistance I might depend upon, and having given me his direction, followed me to the door, where he told me I need not give myself the trouble to call at his house any more, for Mr. Staytape would do my business. At that instant my fellow-dependant coming out after me, overheard the discourse of Mr. Cringer, and making up to me in the street, accosted me very civilly. This address I looked upon as no small honor, considering the figure he made; for he was dressed in a blue frock with a gold button, a green silk waistcoat trimmed with gold, black velvet breeches, while silk stockings, silver buckles, a gold-laced hat, a Spencer wig, and a silver-hilted hanger, with a fine clouded cane in his hand.

"I perceive," says he, "you are but lately come from Scotland; pray what may your business with

I—9

Mr. Cringer be? I suppose it is no secret—and
I may possibly give you some advice that may be
serviceable; for I have been surgeon's second
mate on board of a seventy-gun ship, and consequently know a good deal of the world.'' I made
no scruple to disclose my situation, which when
he had learned, he shook his head, and told me
he had been pretty much in the same circumstances about a year ago; that he had relied on
Cringer's promises, until his money (which was
considerable), as well as his credit, was quite exhausted; and when he wrote to his relations for a
fresh supply, instead of money, he received nothing but reproaches, and the epithets of ''idle,''
''debauched fellow'': that, after he had waited at
the Navy Office many months for a warrant, to
no purpose, he was fain to pawn some of his
clothes, which raised a small sum, wherewith he
bribed the secretary, who soon procured a warrant for him, notwithstanding he had affirmed the
same day, that there was not one vacancy: that
he had gone on board, where he remained nine
months; at the end of which the ship was put out
of commission; and he said the company were to
be paid off in Broad Street the very next day:
that his relations, being reconciled to him, had
charged him to pay his devoirs regularly to Mr.
Cringer, who had informed them by letter that his
interest alone had procured the warrant; in obedience to which command, he came to his levee every
morning as I saw, though he looked upon him to
be a very pitiful scoundrel. In conclusion, he
asked me if I had yet passed at Surgeons' Hall?

To which question I answered, I did not so much
as know it was necessary. "Necessary!" cried
he, "O Lord, O Lord! I find I must instruct you
—come along with me, and I'll give you some information about that matter." So saying, he carried me into an alehouse, where he called for some
beer, and bread and cheese, on which we breakfasted. While we sat in this place, he told me I
must first go to the Navy Office, and write to the
board, desiring them to order a letter for me to
the Surgeons' Hall, that I might be examined
touching my skill in surgery: that the surgeons,
after having examined me, would give me my
qualification sealed up in form of a letter directed
to the commissioners, which qualification I must
deliver to the secretary of the board, who would
open it in my presence, and read the contents.
After which I must employ my interest to be provided for as soon as possible. That the expense
of this qualification, for second mate of a third-
rate, amounted to thirteen shillings, exclusive of
the warrant, which cost him half a guinea and half
a crown, besides the present to the secretary,
which consisted of a three-pound-twelve piece.

This calculation was like a thunderbolt to me,
whose whole fortune did not amount to twelve
shillings. I accordingly made him acquainted
with this part of my distress, after having thanked
him for his information and advice. He condoled
me on this occasion; but bade me be of good cheer,
for he had conceived a friendship for me, and
would make all things easy. He was run out at
present, but to-morrow or next day he was cer-

tain of receiving a considerable sum, of which
he would lend me what would be sufficient to
answer my exigencies. This frank declaration
pleased me so much, that I pulled out my purse,
and emptied it before him, begging him to take
what he pleased for pocket expense, until he
should receive his own money. With a good deal
of pressing he was prevailed upon to take five
shillings, telling me that he might have what
money he wanted at any time for the trouble of
going into the city; but as he had met with me,
he would defer his going thither till to-morrow,
when I should go along with him, and he would
put me in a way of acting for myself, without any
servile dependence on that rascal Cringer, much
less on the lousy tailor to whom I heard him turn
you over. "How," cried I; "is Mr. Staytape a
tailor?" "No less, I'll assure you," answered
he; "and, I confess, more likely to serve you than
the member; for, provided you can entertain him
with politics and conundrums, you may have
credit with him for as many and as rich clothes
as you please. I told him, I was utterly ignorant
of both, and so incensed at Cringer's usage, that
I would never set foot within his door again.
After a good deal more conversation, my new acquaintance and I parted, having made an appointment to meet the next day at the same place, in
order to set out for the city. I went immediately
to Strap, and related everything which had happened; but he did not at all approve of my being
so forward to lend money to a stranger, especially

as we had already been so much imposed upon
by appearances. "However," said he, "if you
are sure he is a Scotchman, I believe you are
safe."

CHAPTER SIXTEEN

IN the morning I rose and went to the place of
rendezvous, where I waited two hours in
vain; and was so exasperated against him
for breaking his appointment, that I set out for
the city by myself, in hopes of finding the villain,
and being revenged on him for his breach of
promise. At length I found myself at the Navy
Office, which I entered, and saw crowds of young
fellows walking below, many of whom made no
better appearance than myself. I consulted the
physiognomy of each, and at last made up to one
whose countenance I liked; and asked if he could
instruct me in the form of the letter which was
to be sent to the board, to obtain an order for examination. He answered me in broad Scotch,
that he would show me the copy of what he had
writ for himself, by the direction of another who
knew the form; and accordingly pulled it out of
his pocket for my perusal; and told me that, if I

was expeditious, I might send it in to the board before dinner, for they did no business in the afternoon. He then went with me to a coffee-house hard by, where I wrote the letter, which was immediately delivered to the messenger; who told me I might expect an order to-morrow about the same time. Having transacted this piece of business, my mind was a good deal composed; and as I met with so much civility from this stranger, I desired further acquaintance with him, fully resolved, however, not to be deceived by him so much to my prejudice as I had been by the beau. He agreed to dine with me at the cook's shop which I frequented; and on our way thither, carried me to 'Change, where I was in some hopes of finding Mr. Jackson (for that was the name of the person who had broke his appointment).

I sought him there to no purpose, and on our way toward the other end of the town, imparted to my companion his behavior toward me. Upon which, he gave me to understand, that he was no stranger to the name of Beau Jackson (so he was called at the Navy Office), although he did not know him personally; that he had the character of a good-natured careless fellow, who made no scruple of borrowing from anybody that would lend; that most people who knew him believed he had a good principle at bottom; but his extravagance was such, he would probably never have it in his power to manifest the honesty of his intention. This account made me sweat for my five shillings, which I nevertheless did not altogether despair of recovering, provided I could find out

the debtor. This young man likewise added another circumstance of Squire Jackson's history,
which was, that being destitute of all means to
equip himself for sea, when he received his last
warrant, he had been recommended to a person
who lent him a little money, after he had signed
a will and power, entitling that person to lift his
wages when they should become due, as also to
inherit his effects in case of his death. That he
was still under the tutorage and direction of that
gentleman, who advanced him small sums from
time to time upon his security at the rate of 50
per cent. But at present his credit was very low,
because his funds would do little more than pay
what he had already received, this moderate interest included. After the stranger (whose name
was Thomson) had entertained me with this account of Jackson, he informed me that he himself
had passed for third mate of a third-rate, about
four months ago; since which time, he had constantly attended at the Navy Office in hope of a
warrant, having been assured from the beginning,
both by a Scotch member and one of the commissioners to whom the member recommended him,
that he should be put into the first vacancy; notwithstanding which promise, he had the mortification to see six or seven appointed to the same station almost every week: that now, being utterly
impoverished, his sole hope consisted in the promise of a friend lately come to town, to lend him a
small matter, for a present to the secretary, without which he was persuaded he might wait a thousand years to no purpose. I conceived a mighty

liking for this young fellow, which, I believe, proceeded from the similitude of our fortunes. We spent the whole day together; and, as he lived at Wapping, I desired him to take a share of my bed.

Next day we returned to the Navy Office, where, after being called before the board, and questioned about the place of my nativity and education, they ordered a letter to be made out for me, which, upon paying half a crown to the clerk, I received, and delivered into the hands of the clerk at Surgeons' Hall, together with a shilling for his trouble in registering my name. By this time my whole stock was diminished to two shillings, and I saw not the least prospect of relief, even for present subsistence, much less to enable me to pay the fees at Surgeons' Hall for my examination, which would come on in a fortnight. In this state of perplexity, I consulted Strap, who assured me, he would pawn everything he had in the world, even to his razors, before I should want. But this expedient I absolutely rejected, telling him, I would a thousand times rather list for a soldier, of which I had some thoughts, than be any longer a burden to him. At the word soldier, he grew pale as death, and begged, on his knees, I would think no more of that scheme. "God preserve us all in our right wits!" cried he, "would you turn soldier, and perhaps be sent abroad against the Spaniards, where you must stand and be shot at like a woodcock?—Heaven keep cold lead out of my carcass! and let me die in a bed like a Christian, as all my forefathers have done. What

signifies all the riches and honors of this life, if
one enjoys not content? And, in the next, there
is no respect of persons. Better be a poor honest
barber with a good conscience, and time to repent
of my sins upon my deathbed, than be cut off
(God bless us) by a musket shot, as it were in
the very flower of one's age, in the pursuit of
riches and fame. What signify riches, my dear
friend? do not they make unto themselves wings?
as the wise man saith; and does not Horace observe, *Non domus et fundus, non æris acervus et
auri, Ægroto domini deduxit corpore febres, Non
animo curas?* I could moreover mention many
other sayings in contempt of riches, both from
the Bible and other good books; but, as I know
you are not very fond of those things, I shall only
assure you that, if you take on to be a soldier, I
will do the same; and then if we should both be
slain, you will not only have your own blood
to answer for, but mine also; and peradventure
the lives of all those whom we shall kill in battle. Therefore, I pray you, consider whether you
will sit down contented with small things, and
share the fruits of my industry in peace, till Providence shall send better tidings; or, by your despair, plunge both our souls and bodies into ever-
lasting perdition, which God of his infinite mercy
forbid." I could not help smiling at this
harangue, which was delivered with great earnestness, the tears standing in his eyes all the time;
and promised to do nothing of that sort without
his consent and concurrence. He was much com-
forted with this declaration; and told me in a few

days he should receive a week's wages, which should be at my service; but advised me, in the meantime, to go in quest of Jackson, and recover, if possible, what he had borrowed of me.

I accordingly trudged about from one end of the town to the other for several days, without being able to learn anything certain concerning him; and, one day, being extremely hungry, and allured by the steams that regaled my nostrils from a boiling cellar, I went down with an intention to gratify my appetite with twopennyworth of beef; when, to my no small surprise, I found Mr. Jackson sitting at dinner with a footman. He no sooner perceived me than he got up and shook me by the hand, saying, he was glad to see me, for he intended to have called at my lodgings in the afternoon. I was so well pleased with this rencounter, and the apologies he made for not keeping his appointment, that I forgot my resentment, and sat down to dinner, with the happy expectation of not only recovering my own money before we should part, but also of reaping the benefit of his promise to lend me wherewithal to pass examination; and this hope my sanguine complexion suggested, though the account Thomson gave me of him ought to have moderated my expectation. When we had feasted sumptuously, he took his leave of the footman, and adjourned with me to an alehouse hard by, where, after shaking me by the hand again, he began thus: "I suppose you think me a sad dog, Mr. Random, and I do confess that appearances are against me. But I daresay you will forgive me, when I tell you, my not coming

at the time appointed was owing to a peremptory
message I received from a certain lady, whom,
harkee, (but this is a great secret,) I am to marry
very soon. You think this strange, perhaps, but
it is not less true for all that—a five thousand
pounder. I'll assure you, besides expectations.
For my own part, devil take me if I know what
any woman can see engaging about me—but a
whim, you know; and then one would not balk
one's good fortune. You saw that footman who
dined with us—he's one of the honestest fellows
that ever wore a livery. You must know, it was
by his means I was introduced to her, for he made
me first acquainted with her woman, who is his
mistress; ay, many a crown has he and his sweetheart had of my money; but what of that? things
are now brought to a bearing. I have—come a
little this way—I have proposed marriage, and
the day is fixed; she's a charming creature; writes
like an angel. O Lord! she can repeat all the
English tragedies as well as e'er a player in
Drury Lane! and indeed is so fond of plays, that,
to be near the stage, she has taken lodgings in a
court hard by the theater. But you shall see—
you shall see—here's the last letter she sent me.''
—With these words, he put into my hand, and I
read, to the best of my remembrance, as follows:—

"DEER KREETER,—As you are the animable hopjack of
my contemplayshins, your aydear is infernally skimming
before my keymerycal fansee, when Murfy sends his puppies
to the heys of slipping mortals; and when Febus shines
from his merrydying throne. Whereupon, I shall canseeif
old whorie time has lost his pinners, as also Cupid his har-

rows, until thou enjoy sweet propose in the loafseek harms
of thy faithfool to command,   CLAYRENDER."
  "Wingar-yeard, Droory-lane,
        January 12th."

While I was reading, he seemed to be in an
ecstasy, rubbing his hands, and bursting out into
fits of laughter; at last he caught hold of my hand,
and, squeezing it, cried, "There is style for you!
what do you think of this billet-doux?" I answered, "It might be sublime for aught I knew,
for it was altogether above my comprehension."
—"Oho!" said he, "I believe it is both tender
and sublime—she's a divine creature!—and so
doats upon me! Let me see, what shall I do with
this money, when I have once got it into my
hands? In the first place, I shall do for you—I'm
a man of few words; but, say no more, that's determined—whether would you advise me to purchase some post, by which I may rise in the state;
or lay out my wife's fortune in land, and retire
to the country at once?"—I gave my opinion without hesitation, that he could not do better than
buy an estate and improve; especially since he
had already seen so much of the world. Then I
launched out into the praises of a country life, as
described by the poets whose works I had read.
He seemed to relish my advice, but withal told
me, that, although he had seen a great deal of the
world, both by land and sea, having cruised three
whole months in the Channel, yet he should not
be satisfied until he had visited France, which
he proposed to do before he should settle; and
to carry his wife along with him.

I had nothing to object to his proposal; and asked how soon he hoped to be happy? "As to that," he replied, "nothing obstructs my happiness, but the want of a little ready cash; for you must know, my friend in the city has gone out of town for a week or two; and I unfortunately missed my pay at Broad Street, by being detained too long by the dear charmer; but there will be a recall at Chatham next week, whither the ship's books are sent, and I have commissioned a friend in that place to receive the money." "If that be all," said I, "there's no great harm in deferring your marriage a few days."—"Yes, faith! but there is," said he; "you don't know how many rivals I have, who would take all advantages against me. I would not balk the impatience of her passion for the world; the least appearance of coldness and indifference would ruin all: and such offers don't occur every day." I acquiesced in this observation, and inquired how he intended to proceed: at this question, he rubbed his chin, and said, "Why, truly, I must be obliged to some friend or other—do you know of nobody that would lend me a small sum for a day or two?"— I assured him, I was such an utter stranger in London, that I did not believe I could borrow a guinea if my life depended upon it. "No!" said he, "that's hard—that's hard. I wish I had anything to pawn; upon my soul you have got excellent linen (feeling the sleeve of my shirt); how many shirts of that kind have you got?"—I answered, "Six ruffled and six plain";—at which he testified great surprise, and swore that no gentle-

man ought to have more than four. "How many
d'ye think I have got?" continued he. "But this
and another, as I hope to be saved! I daresay we
shall be able to raise a good sum out of your
superfluity—let me see—let me see—each of these
shirts is worth sixteen shillings at a moderate
computation; now suppose we pawn them for half
price, eight times eight is sixty-four, that's three
pounds four; zounds! that will do; give me your
hand.—"Softly, softly, Mr. Jackson," said I,
"don't dispose of my linen without my consent;
first pay me the crown you owe me, and then we
shall talk of other matters." He protested he had
not above one shilling in his pocket, but that he
would pay me out of the first of the money
raised from the shirts.

This piece of assurance incensed me so much,
that I swore I would not part with him until I
had received satisfaction for what I had lent him;
and, as for the shirts, I would not pawn one of
them to save him from the gallows. At this expression, he laughed aloud, and then complained
it was d—n'd hard, that I should refuse him a
trifle that would infallibly enable him not only to
make his own fortune, but mine also. "You talk
of pawning my shirts," said I, "suppose you
should sell this hanger, Mr. Jackson? I believe it
would fetch a good round sum."—"No, hang it,"
said he, "I can't appear decently without my
hanger, or egad it should go." However, seeing
me inflexible with regard to my linen, he at length
unbuckled his hanger, and, showing me the sign
of the three blue balls, desired me to carry it

thither and pawn it for two guineas. This office I would by no means have performed, had I seen any likelihood of having my money otherwise; but not willing, out of a piece of false delicacy, to neglect the only opportunity I should perhaps ever have, I ventured into a pawnbroker's shop, where I demanded two guineas on the pledge, in the name of Thomas Williams. "Two guineas!" said the pawnbroker, looking at the hanger; "this piece of goods has been here several times before for thirty shillings; however, since I believe the gentleman to whom it belongs will redeem it, he shall have what he wants"; and accordingly, he paid me the money, which I carried to the house where I had left Jackson, and, calling for change, counted out to him seven and thirty shillings, reserving the other five for myself.

After looking at the money some time, he said, "D—n it! it don't signify—this won't do my business; so you may as well take half a guinea, or a whole one, as the five shillings you have kept." I thanked him kindly; but I refused to accept of any more than was my due, because I had no prospect of repaying it. Upon which declaration, he stared in my face, and told me, I was excessively raw, or I would not talk in that manner. "Blood," cried he, "I have a very bad opinion of a young fellow who won't borrow of his friend when he is in want; 'tis the sign of a sneaking spirit. Come, come, Random, give me back the five shillings, and take this half-guinea, and if ever you are able to pay me, I believe you will; if not, d—n me if I ever ask it." When I

reflected on my present necessity, I suffered myself to be persuaded; and, after making my ac-
knowledgments to Mr. Jackson, who offered to
treat me with a play, I returned to my lodgings
with a much better opinion of this gentleman
than I had in the morning; and at night imparted
my day's adventures to Strap, who rejoiced at the
good luck, saying, "I told you, if he was a Scotchman, you was safe enough; and who knows but
this marriage may make us all? You have heard,
I suppose, as how a countryman of ours, a journeyman baker, ran away with a great lady of this
town, and now keeps his coach. Ecod! I say
nothing; but yesterday morning, as I was a shav-
ing a gentleman at his own house, there was a
young lady in the room—a fine buxom wench,
i'faith! and she threw so many sheep's eyes at
a certain person whom I shall not name, that my
heart went knock, knock, knock, like a fulling mill,
and my hand sh—sh—shook so much that I sliced
a piece of skin off the gentleman's nose. Whereby
he swore a deadly oath, and was going to horse-
whip me, when she prevented him, and made my
peace. *Omen haud malum!* Is not a journeyman barber as good as a journeyman baker? The
only difference is, the baker uses flour for the
belly, and the barber uses it for the head. And
as the head is a more noble member than the
belly, so is a barber more noble than a baker; for
what's the belly without the head? Besides, I am
told he could neither read nor write; now you
know I can do both, and, moreover, speak Latin.
But I will say no more, for I despise vanity; noth-

ing is more vain than vanity.'' With these words he pulled out of his pocket a wax candle's end, which he applied to his forehead; and, upon examination, I found he had combed his own hair over the toupee of his wig, and was indeed in his whole dress become a very smart shaver. I congratulated him on his prospect with a satirical smile, which he understood very well; and, shaking his head, observed I had very little faith, but the truth would come to light in spite of my incredulity.

CHAPTER SEVENTEEN

I go to Surgeons' Hall, where I meet with Mr. Jackson—Am
examined—A fierce Dispute arises between two of the
Examiners—Jackson disguises himself to attract Respect—Is detected—In hazard of being sent to Bridewell
—He treats us at a Tavern—Carries us to a Night House
—A troublesome Adventure there—We are committed
to the Round House—Carried before a Justice—His Behavior.

WITH the assistance of this faithful ad-
herent, who gave me almost all the
money he earned, I preserved my half-
guinea entire till the day of examination, when I
went with a quaking heart to Surgeons' Hall, in
order to undergo that ceremony. Among a crowd
of young fellows who walked in the outward hall,
I perceived Mr. Jackson, to whom I immediately
went up, and inquiring into the state of his amour,
understood it was still undetermined by reason of
his friend's absence, and the delay of the recall
at Chatham, which put it out of his power to
bring it to a conclusion. I then asked what his
business was in this place? he replied, he was resolved to have two strings to his bow, that in case
the one failed he might use the other; and, with
this view, he was to pass that night for a higher
qualification. At that instant a young fellow
came out from the place of examination with a
pale countenance, his lip quivering, and his looks

147

as wild as if he had seen a ghost. He no sooner appeared, than we all flocked about him with the utmost eagerness to know what reception he had met with; which, after some pause, he described, recounting all the questions they had asked, with the answers he made. In this manner, we obliged no less than twelve to recapitulate, which, now the danger was past, they did with pleasure, before it fell to my lot: at length the beadle called my name, with a voice that made me tremble as much as if it had been the sound of the last trumpet: however, there was no remedy: I was conducted into a large hall, where I saw about a dozen of grim faces sitting at a long table; one of whom bade me come forward, in such an imperious tone that I was actually for a minute or two bereft of my senses. The first question he put to me was, "Where was you born?" To which I answered, "In Scotland."—"In Scotland," said he; "I know that very well; we have scarce any other countrymen to examine here; you Scotchmen have overspread us of late as the locusts did Egypt: I ask you in what part of Scotland was you born?" I named the place of my nativity, which he had never before heard of: he then proceeded to interrogate me about my age, the town where I served my time, with the term of my apprenticeship; and when I informed him that I served three years only, he fell into a violent passion; swore it was a shame and a scandal to send such raw boys into the world as surgeons; that it was a great presumption in me, and an affront upon the English, to pretend to sufficient skill in my

business, having served so short a time, when
every apprentice in England was bound seven
years at least; that my friends would have done
better if they had made me a weaver or shoemaker, but their pride would have me a gentleman, he supposed at any rate, and their poverty
could not afford the necessary education.

This exordium did not at all contribute to the
recovery of my spirits, but, on the contrary, reduced me to such a situation that I was scarce able
to stand; which being perceived by a plump gentleman who sat opposite to me, with a skull before him, he said, Mr. Snarler was too severe upon
the young man; and, turning toward me, told me,
I need not to be afraid, for nobody would do me
any harm; then bidding me take time to recollect myself, he examined me touching the opera-
tions of the trepan, and was very well satisfied
with my answers. The next person who questioned me was a wag, who began by asking if I
had ever seen amputation performed; and I replying in the affirmative, he shook his head, and
said, "What! upon a dead subject, I suppose?"
"If," continued he, "during an engagement at
sea, a man should be brought to you with his head
shot off, how would you behave?" After some
hesitation, I owned such a case had never come
under my observation, neither did I remember to
have seen any method of cure proposed for such
an accident, in any of the systems of surgery I
had perused. Whether it was owing to the simplicity of my answer, or the archness of the question, I know not, but every member of the board

deigned to smile, except Mr. Snarler, who seemed
to have very little of the *animal risibile* in his constitution. The facetious member, encouraged by
the success of his last joke, went on thus: ''Suppose you was called to a patient of a plethoric
habit, who had been bruised by a fall, what would
you do?'' I answered, I would bleed him immediately. ''What,'' said he, ''before you had tied
up his arm?'' But this stroke of wit not answering his expectation, he desired me to advance to
the gentleman who sat next him; and who, with
a pert air, asked what method of cure I would
follow in wounds of the intestines. I repeated
the method of cure as it is prescribed by the best
chirurgical writers; which he heard to an end,
and then said, with a supercilious smile, ''So you
think by such treatment the patient might recover?''—I told him I saw nothing to make me
think otherwise. ''That may be,'' resumed he,
''I won't answer for your foresight; but did you
ever know a case of this kind succeed''; I answered I did not; and was about to tell him I had
never seen a wounded intestine; but he stopped
me, by saying, with some precipitation, ''Nor
never will. I affirm, that all wounds of the intestines, whether great or small, are mortal.''—
''Pardon me, brother,'' says the fat gentleman,
''there is very good authority.''—Here he was interrupted by the other, with ''Sir, excuse me, I
despise all authority. *Nullius in verba*. I stand
upon my own bottom.''—''But, sir, sir,'' replied
his antagonist, ''the reason of the thing shows.''
—''A fig for reason,'' cried this sufficient mem-

ber, "I laugh at reason; give me ocular demon-
stration." The corpulent gentleman began to
wax warm, and observed, that no man acquainted
with the anatomy of the parts would advance
such an extravagant assertion. This innuendo
enraged the other so much, that he started up,
and in a furious tone, exclaimed, "What, sir! do
you question my knowledge in anatomy?" By
this time, all the examiners had espoused the opinion of one or other of the disputants, and raised
their voices all together, when the chairman commanded silence, and ordered me to withdraw. In
less than a quarter of an hour I was called in
again, received my qualification sealed up, and
was ordered to pay five shillings.

I laid down my half-guinea upon the table, and
stood some time, until one of them bade me be-
gone; to this I replied, "I will, when I get my
change"; upon which another threw me five shillings and sixpence, saying, I should not be a true
Scotchman if I went away without my change.
I was afterwards obliged to give three shillings
and sixpence to the beadles, and a shilling to an
old woman who swept the hall. This disburse-
ment sunk my finances to thirteenpence halfpenny,
with which I was sneaking off, when Jackson perceiving it, came up to me, and begged I would
tarry for him, and he would accompany me to the
other end of the town, as soon as his examination
should be over. I could not refuse this to a person that was so much my friend; but I was astonished at the change of his dress, which was
varied in half an hour from what I have already

described, to a very grotesque fashion. His head
was covered with an old smoked tie wig that did
not boast one crooked hair, and a slouched hat
over it, which would have very well become a
chimney-sweeper or a dustman; his neck was
adorned with a black crape, the ends of which he
had twisted, and fixed in the button-hole of a
shabby great-coat that wrapped up his whole
body; his white silk stockings were converted into
black worsted hose; and his countenance was rendered venerable by wrinkles, and a beard of his
own painting.

When I expressed my surprise at this meta-
morphosis, he laughed, and told me, it was done
by the advice and assistance of a friend who
lived over the way, and would certainly produce
something very much to his advantage; for it gave
him the appearance of age, which never fails of
attracting respect. I applauded his sagacity, and
waited with impatience for the effects of it. At
length he was called in, but whether the oddness
of his appearance excited a curiosity more than
usual in the board, or his behavior was not suitable to his figure, I know not; he was discovered
to be an impostor, and put into the hands of the
beadle, in order to be sent to Bridewell. So that
instead of seeing him come out with a cheerful
countenance, and a surgeon's qualification in his
hand, I perceived him led through the outward
hall as a prisoner, and was very much alarmed
and anxious to know the occasion; when he called
with a lamentable voice and piteous aspect to me,
and some others who knew him, "For God's sake,

gentlemen, bear witness that I am the same individual John Jackson, who served as surgeon's
second mate on board the *Elizabeth*, or else I shall
go to Bridewell.'' It would have been impossible
for the most austere hermit that ever lived to have
refrained from laughing at his appearance and
address; we therefore indulged ourselves a good
while at his expense, and afterwards pleaded his
cause so effectually with the beadle, who was
gratified with half a crown, that the prisoner was
dismissed, and, in a few moments, resumed his
former gaiety; swearing, since the board had refused his money, he would spend it every shilling
before he went to bed in treating his friends; at
the same time inviting us all to favor him with
our company. It was now ten o'clock at night,
and as I had a great way to walk, through streets
that were utterly unknown to me, I was prevailed
upon to be of their party, in hopes he would afterward accompany me to my lodgings, according to
his promise.

He conducted us to his friend's house, who kept
a tavern over the way, where we continued drinking punch, until the liquor mounted up to our
heads, and made us all extremely frolicsome: I
in particular was so much elevated, that nothing
would serve me but a wench, at which demand
Jackson expressed much joy, and assured me I
should have my desire before we parted. Accordingly, when we had paid the reckoning, we sallied
out, roaring and singing; and were conducted by
our leader to a place of nocturnal entertainment,
where I immediately attached myself to a fair

one, with whom I proposed to spend the remaining part of the night; but she not relishing my appearance, refused to grant my request before I should have made her an acknowledgment; which not suiting with my circumstances, we broke off our correspondence, to my no small mortification and resentment, because I thought the mercenary creature had not done justice to my merit.   In the meantime, Mr. Jackson's dress had attracted the inclinations and assiduities of two or three nymphs, who loaded him with caresses, in return for the arrack punch with which he treated them; till at length, notwithstanding the sprightly sallies of those charmers, sleep began to exert his power over us all; and our conductor called, "To pay." When the bill was brought, which amounted to twelve shillings, he put his hand in his pocket, but might have saved himself the trouble, for his purse was gone.   This accident disconcerted him a great deal at first; but, after some recollection, he seized the two Dulcineas who sat by him, one in each hand, and swore, if they did not immediately restore his money, he would charge a constable with them.

The good lady at the bar, seeing what had passed, whispered something to the drawer, who went out; and then, with great composure, asked what was the matter?   Jackson told her he was robbed, and swore, if she refused him satisfaction, he would have her and her whores committed to Bridewell.   "Robbed," cried she, "robbed in my house!   Gentlemen and ladies, I take you all to witness, this person has scandalized my reputa-

tion.'' At that instant seeing the constable and
watch enter, she proceeded, ''What! you must not
only endeavor by your false aspersions to ruin
my character, but even commit an assault upon
my family! Mr. Constable, I charge you with
this uncivil person, who has been guilty of a riot
here; I shall take care and bring an action against
him for defamation.'' While I was reflecting on
this melancholy event, which had made me quite
sober, the lady whose favors I had solicited, being piqued at some repartee that passed between
us, cried, ''They are all concerned''; and desired
the constable to take us all into custody; an ar-
rest which was performed instantly, to the utter
astonishment and despair of us all, except Jackson, who having been often in such scrapes, was
very little concerned, and charged the constable
in his turn with the landlady and her whole bevy:
upon which we were carried all together prisoners
to the Round House; where Jackson, after a word
of comfort to us, informed the constable of his
being robbed, to which he said he would swear
next morning before the justice. ''Ay, ay,'' says
the bawd, ''we shall see whose oath will most signify.'' In a little time, the constable, calling
Jackson into another room, spoke to him thus:
''I perceive that you and your company are
strangers, and am very sorry for your being
involved in such an ugly business. I have known
this woman a great while; she has kept a notorious house in the neighborhood this many years,
and, although often complained of as a nuisance,
still escapes, through her interest with the jus-

tices, to whom she, and all of her employment, pay
contribution quarterly for protection. As she
charged me with you first, her complaint will have
the preference; and she can procure evidence to
swear whatever she shall please to desire of
them. So that unless you can make it up before
morning, you and your companions may think
yourselves happily quit for a month's hard labor
in Bridewell. Nay, if she should swear a robbery
or assault against you, you will be committed to
Newgate, and tried next sessions at the Old Bailey
for your life.'' This last piece of information
had such an effect upon Jackson, that he agreed
to make it up, provided his money might be restored. The constable told him, that, instead of
retrieving what he had lost, he was pretty certain
it would cost him some more before they would
come to any composition. But, however, he had
compassion on him, and would, if he pleased,
sound them about a mutual release. The unfortunate beau thanked him for his friendship,
and returning to us, acquainted us with the sub-
stance of this dialogue; while the constable, desiring to speak in private with our adversary, carried her into the next room, and pleaded our
cause so effectually, that she condescended to
make him umpire: he accordingly proposed an
arbitration, to which we gave our assent; and he
fined each party in three shillings, to be laid out
in a bowl of punch, wherein we drowned all animosities, to the inexpressible joy of my two late
acquaintances and me, who had been in the state

of the damned ever since Jackson mentioned
Bridewell and Newgate. By the time we had finished our bowl, to which, by the by, I had con-
tributed my last shilling, it was morning; and I
proposed to move homeward, when the constable
gave me to understand, he could discharge no
prisoners, but by order of the justice, before
whom we must appear. This renewed my chagrin; and I cursed the hour in which I had yielded
to Jackson's invitation. About nine o'clock we
were escorted to the house of a certain justice, not
many miles distant from Covent Garden; who no
sooner saw the constable enter with a train of
prisoners at his heels, than he saluted him as follows: "So, Mr. Constable, you are a diligent
man—What den of rogues have you been scour-
ing?" Then looking at us, who appeared very
much dejected, he continued, "Ay, ay, thieves, I
see—old offenders—O your humble servant, Mrs.
Harridan! I suppose these fellows have been
taken robbing your house—yes, yes, here's an old
acquaintance of mine—you have used expedition," said he to me, "in returning from transportation; but we shall save you the trouble for
the future—the surgeons will fetch you from your
next transportation at their expense." I assured
his worship he was mistaken in me, for he had
never seen me in his life before. To this declaration he replied, "How! you impudent rascal, dare
you say so to my face? Do you think I am to be
imposed upon by that northern accent which you
have assumed? but it shan't avail you—you shall

find me too far north for you. Here, clerk, write this fellow's *mittimus*. His name is Patrick Gahagan.''

Here Mr. Jackson interposed, and told him I was a Scotchman lately come to town, descended of a good family, and that my name was Random. The justice looked upon this assertion as an outrage upon his memory, on which he valued himself much; and strutting up to Jackson, with a fierce countenance, put his hands in his sides and said, ''Who are you, sir? Do you give me the lie? Take notice, gentlemen, here's a fellow who affronts me upon the bench; but I'll lay you fast, sirrah, I will; for notwithstanding your laced jacket, I believe you are a notorious felon.'' My friend was so much abashed at this menace, which was thundered out with great vociferation, that he changed color, and remained speechless. This confusion his worship took for a symptom of guilt, and to complete his discovery, continued his threats—''Now, I am convinced you are a thief—your face discovers it—you tremble all over—your conscience won't lie still—you'll be hanged, sirrah,'' raising his voice, ''you'll be hanged; and happy had it been for the world, as well as your own miserable soul, if you had been detected and cut off in the beginning of your career. Come hither, clerk, and take this man's confession.'' I was in an agony of consternation, when the constable, going into another room with his worship, acquainted him with the truth of the story; which having learned, he returned with a smiling countenance, and addressing himself to us all, said it was always his way to terrify young people, when they came before him, that his threats might make a strong impression on their minds, and deter them from engaging in scenes of riot and debauchery, which commonly ended before the judge. Thus having cloaked his own want of discernment under the disguise of paternal care, we were dismissed, and I found myself as much lightened as if a mountain had been lifted off my breast.

CHAPTER EIGHTEEN

I WOULD willingly have gone home to sleep, but was told by my companions, that we must deliver our letters of qualification at the Navy Office before one o'clock; accordingly we went thither, and gave them to the secretary, who opened and read them; and I was mightily pleased to find myself qualified for second mate of a third-rate. When he had stuck them altogether on a file, one of our company asked if there were any vacancies? to which interrogation he answered, No. Then I ventured to inquire if any ships were to be put in commission soon? At which question he surveyed me with a look of ineffable contempt, and, pushing us out of his office, locked the door, without deigning us another word. We went downstairs, and conferred together on our expectations, when I understood that each of them had been recommended to one or other of the commissioners, and each of them promised the first vacancy that should fall; but that none of them relied solely upon that interest, without a present

to the secretary, with whom some of the commissioners went snacks. For which reason each of
them had provided a small purse; and I was asked
what I proposed to give?

This was a vexatious question to me, who, far
from being in a capacity to gratify a ravenous
secretary, had not wherewithal to purchase a dinner. I therefore answered, I had not yet determined what to give; and sneaked off toward my
own lodgings, cursing my fate all the way, and
inveighing with much bitterness against the barbarity of my grandfather, and the sordid avarice
of my relations, who left me a prey to contempt
and indigence. Full of these disagreeable reflec-
tions, I arrived at the house where I lodged, and
relieved my landlord from great anxiety on my
account; for this honest man believed I had met
with some dismal accident, and that he should
never see me again. Strap, who had come to
visit me in the morning, understanding I had been
abroad all night, was almost distracted, and, after
having obtained leave of his master, had gone
in quest of me, though he was even more ignorant
of the town than I. Not being willing to inform
my landlord of my adventure, I told him I had
met with an acquaintance at Surgeons' Hall, with
whom I spent the evening and night, but being
very much infested by bugs, I had not slept much,
and therefore intended to take a little repose; so
saying, I went to bed, and desired to be awakened,
if Strap should happen to come while I should be
asleep. I was accordingly roused by my friend
himself, who entered my chamber about three
I—11

o'clock in the afternoon; and presented a figure
to my eyes, that I could scarce believe real. In
short, this affectionate shaver, setting out toward
Surgeons' Hall, had inquired for me there to no
purpose; from thence he found his way to the
Navy Office, where he could hear no tidings of
me, because I was unknown to everybody then
present; he afterward went upon 'Change, in
hopes of seeing me upon the Scotch walk, but
without success.

At last, being almost in despair of finding me,
he resolved to ask everybody he met in the street,
if perchance anyone could give him information
about me; and actually put his resolution in practice, in spite of the scoffs, curses, and reproaches
with which he was answered; until a blacksmith's
'prentice, seeing him stop a porter with a burden
on his back, and hearing his question, for which
he received a hearty curse, called to him, and
asked if the person he inquired after was not a
Scotchman? Strap replied with great eagerness, "Yes, and had on a brown coat with long
skirts." "The same," said the blacksmith, "I
saw him pass by an hour ago." "Did you so?"
cried Strap, rubbing his hands, "Odd! I am very
glad of that—which way went he?" "Towards
Tyburn in a cart," said he; "if you make good
speed, you may get thither time enough to see him
hanged." This piece of wit incensed my friend
to such a degree, that he called the blacksmith
scoundrel, and protested he would fight him for
half a farthing. "No, no," said the other, stripping, "I'll have none of your money—you Scotch-

men seldom carry any about with you—but I'll
fight you for love." There was a ring immediately formed by the mob; and Strap finding he
could not get off honorably without fighting, at
the same time burning with resentment against
his adversary, quitted his clothes to the care of
the multitude, and the battle began with great
violence on the side of Strap, who in a few minutes exhausted his breath and spirits on his patient antagonist, who sustained the assault with
great coolness, till, finding the barber quite spent,
he returned the blows he had lent him with such
interest, that Strap, after having received· three
falls on the hard stones, gave out, and allowed
the blacksmith to be the better man.

The victory being thus decided, it was proposed
to adjourn to a cellar hard by, and drink friends.
But when my friend began to gather up his
clothes, he perceived that some honest person or
other had made free with his shirt, neckcloth,
hat, and wig, which were carried off; and probably his coat and waistcoat would have met with
the same fate, had they been worth stealing. It
was in vain for him to make a noise, which only
yielded mirth to the spectators; he was fain to
get off in this manner, which he accomplished
with much difficulty, and appeared before me all
besmeared with blood and dirt. Notwithstanding
this misfortune, such was his transport at finding me safe and sound, that he had almost stifled
and stunk me to death with his embraces. After
he had cleaned himself, and put on one of my
shirts, and a woolen nightcap, I recounted to him

the particulars of my night's campaign, which filled him with admiration and made him repeat with great energy an observation which was often in his mouth, namely, "that surely London is the devil's drawing-room." As neither of us had dined, he desired me to get up; and the milk-woman coming round at that instant, he went downstairs, and brought up a quart, with a penny brick, on which we made a comfortable meal. He then shared his money with me, which amounted to eighteenpence, and left me, with an intention to borrow an old wig and hat of his friend the schoolmaster.

He was no sooner gone, than I began to consider my situation with great uneasiness, and resolved all the schemes my imagination could suggest, in order to choose and pursue some one that might procure me bread; for it is impossible to express the pangs I felt, when I reflected on the miserable dependence in which I lived at the expense of a poor barber's boy. My pride took the alarm, and having no hopes of succeeding at the Navy Office, I came to a resolution of enlisting in the foot-guards next day, be the event what it would. This extravagant design, by flattering my disposition, gave great satisfaction; and I was charging the enemy at the head of my own regiment, when Strap's return interrupted my reverie. The schoolmaster had made him a present of the tie wig which he wore when I was introduced to him, together with an old hat, whose brims would have overshadowed a Colossus. Though Strap had ventured to wear them in the

dusk, he did not choose to entertain the mob by
day; therefore went to work immediately, and reduced them both to a moderate size. While he
was employed in this office, he addressed me thus:
"To be sure, Mr. Random, you are born a gentleman, and have a great deal of learning—and
indeed look like a gentleman; for, as to person,
you may hold up your head with the best of them.
On the other hand, I am a poor but honest cobbler's son—my mother was as industrious a
woman as ever broke bread, till such time as she
took to drinking, which you very well know—but
everybody has failings—*humanum est errare*.
Now, for myself, I am a poor journeyman barber,
tolerably well made, and understand some Latin,
and have a smattering of Greek—but what of
that? perhaps I might also say that I know a little of the world—but that is to no purpose—
though you be gentle and I simple, it does not
follow but that I who am simple may do a good
office to you who are gentle. Now this is the case
—my kinsman the schoolmaster—perhaps you did
not know how nearly he is related to me—I'll
satisfy you in that presently—his mother and
my grandmother's sister's nephew—no, that's not
it—my grandfather's brother's daughter—rabbit
it! I have forgot the degree, but this I know, he
and I are cousins seven times removed." My
impatience to know the good office he had done
me got the better of my temper, and interrupted
him at this place, with, "D—n your relation and
pedigree! if the schoolmaster or you can be of
any advantage to me, why don't you tell me with-

out all this preamble?'' When I pronounced
these words with some vehemence, Strap looked
at me for some time with a grave countenance,
and then went on: ''Surely my pedigree is not
to be d—n'd, because it is not so noble as yours.
I am very sorry to see such an alteration in your
temper of late—you was always fiery, but now
you are grown as crabbed as old Perriwinkle the
drunken tinker, on whom you and I, God forgive
us, played so many unlucky tricks, while we were
at school. But I will no longer detain you in sus-
pense, because, doubtless, nothing is more uneasy
than doubt—*dubio, procul dubio, nil dubius.* My
friend, or relation, or which you will, or both, the
schoolmaster, being informed of the regard I have
for you—for, you may be sure, I did not fail to
let him know your good qualities—by the by, he
has undertaken to teach you the pronunciation of
the English tongue, without which, he says, you
will be unfit for business in this country—I say
my relation has spoke in your behalf to a French
apothecary who wants a journeyman; and, on his
recommendation, you may have fifteen pounds per
year, bed and board, whenever you please.'' I
was too much interested in this piece of news to
entertain it with indifference; but, jumping up,
insisted on Strap's immediately accompanying
me to the house of his friend, that I might not
lose this opportunity through the least delay or
neglect on my part.

We were informed that the schoolmaster was in
company at a public-house in the neighborhood,
whither we repaired, and found him drinking with

the very individual apothecary in question. When he was called to the door at our desire, and observed my impatience, he broke out into his usual term of admiration: "O Ch—st! I suppose, when you heard of this offer, you did not take leisure enough to come downstairs, but leapt out of the window; did you overturn no porter nor oyster-woman in your way! It is a mercy of God you did not knock your brains out against some post in your career. O my conscience! I believe, had I been in the inmost recesses of my habitation,—the very *penetralia,*—even in bed with my wife; your eagerness would have surmounted bolts, bars, decency, and everything. The den of Cacus or *Sanctum Sanctorum* could not have hid me from you. But come along, the gentleman of whom I spoke is in the house, I will present you to him forthwith." When I entered the room, I perceived four or five people smoking, one of whom the schoolmaster accosted thus: "Mr. Lavement, here's the young man of whom I spoke to you." The apothecary, who was a little old withered man, with a forehead about an inch high, a nose turned up at the end, large cheek-bones that helped to form a pit for his little gray eyes, a great bag of loose skin hanging down on each side in wrinkles like the alforjas of a baboon; and a mouth so accustomed to that contraction which produces grinning, that he could not pronounce a syllable without discovering the remains of his teeth, which consisted of four yellow fangs, not improperly, by anatomists, called *canine;*—this person, I say, after having

eyed me some time, said, "Oho, 'tis very well,
Mons. Concordance;—young man, you are ver
welcome, take one coup of bierre—and come to
mine house to-marrow morning: Mons. Concordance vil show you de way." Upon this I made
my bow, and as I went out of the room, could
hear him say, *"Ma foi! ' est un beau garçon, c'est
un galliard."* As I had, by my own application,
while I served Crab, acquired the French tongue
well enough to read authors written in that language, and understand anything that occurred in
conversation, I determined to pretend ignorance
to my new master, that he and his family, whom
I supposed to be of the same country, not being
on the reserve before me, might possibly discover
something in discourse, which would either yield
me amusement or advantage. Next morning Mr.
Concordance carried me to the apothecary's
house, where the bargain was made, and orders
given to provide an apartment for me immediately. But, before I entered upon business, the
schoolmaster recommended me to his tailor, who
gave me credit for a suit of clothes to be paid
out of the first moiety of my wages, and they were
begun upon that very day; he afterward accommodated me with a new hat, on the same terms;
so that, in a few days, I hoped to make a very
fashionable appearance. In the meantime, Strap
conveyed my baggage to the place allotted for me,
which was a back room up two pair of stairs,
furnished with a pallet for me to lie upon, a chair
without a back, an earthen chamber-pot without a
handle, a bottle by way of candlestick, and a tri-

angular piece of glass instead of a mirror, the
rest of its ornaments having been lately removed
to one of the garrets, for the convenience of the
servant of an Irish captain, who lodged in the
first floor.

CHAPTER NINETEEN

The Characters of Mr. Lavement, his Wife and Daughter—
Some Anecdotes of the Family—The Mother and
Daughter rivals—I am guilty of a Mistake that gives
me present Satisfaction, but is attended with troublesome Consequences.

NEXT day, while I was at work in the shop,
a bouncing damsel, well dressed, came in,
on pretense of finding a phial for some
use or other; and taking an opportunity, when
she thought I did not mind her, of observing me
narrowly, went away with a silent look of disdain.
I easily guessed her sentiments, and my pride
took the resolution of entertaining the same indifference and neglect toward her. At dinner,
the maids, with whom I dined in the kitchen, gave
me to understand that this was my master's only
daughter, who would have a very handsome fortune, on account of which, and her beauty, a great
many young gentlemen made their addresses to
her; that she had been twice on the brink of
marriage, but disappointed by the stinginess of
her father, who refused to part with a shilling
to promote the match; for which reason the young
lady did not behave to her father with all the
filial veneration that might be expected. In particular, she harbored the most perfect hatred for
his countrymen, in which disposition she resembled her mother, who was an Englishwoman; and,
170

by the hints they dropped, I learned the gray mare was the better horse; that she was a matron of a high spirit, which was often manifested at the expense of her dependants; that she loved diversions, and looked upon Miss as her rival in all parties; which, indeed, was the true cause of all her disappointments, for, had the mother been hearty in her interest, the father would not have ventured to refuse her demands.

Over and above this intelligence, I, of myself, soon made more discoveries. Mr. Lavement's significant grins at his wife, while she looked another way, convinced me that he was not at all content with his lot; and his behavior in presence of the captain, made me believe his chief torment was jealousy. As for my own part, I was considered in no other light than that of a menial servant, and had been already six days in the house without being honored with one word from either mother or daughter, the latter (as I understood from the maids) having, at table, one day expressed some surprise that her papa should entertain such an awkward mean-looking journeyman. I was nettled at this piece of information, and next Sunday, (it being my turn to take my diversion,) dressed myself in my new clothes, to the greatest advantage, and, vanity apart, made no contemptible figure. After having spent most part of the day in company with Strap, and some of his acquaintance, I came home in the afternoon, and was let in by Miss, who, not knowing me, dropped a low curtsey as I advanced, which I returned with a profound bow, and shut the door.

By the time I had turned about, she had perceived her mistake, and changed color, but did not withdraw. The passage being narrow, I could not get away without jostling her; so I was forced to remain where I was, with my eyes fixed on the ground, and my face glowing with blushes. At length her vanity coming to her assistance, she went away tittering, and I could hear her pronounce the word "Creature." From this day forward, she came into the shop fifty times every day, upon various pretenses, and put in practice so many ridiculous airs, that I could easily perceive her opinion of me was changed, and that she did not think me altogether an unworthy conquest. But my heart was so steeled against her charms by pride and resentment, which were two chief ingredients in my disposition, that I remained insensible to all her arts; and, notwithstanding some advances she made, could not be prevailed upon to yield her the least attention. This neglect soon banished all the favorable impressions she felt for me, and the rage of a slighted woman took place in her heart; this she manifested not only in all the suggestions her malice could invent to my prejudice with her father, but also in procuring for me such servile employments as she hoped would sufficiently humble my spirit. One day, in particular, she ordered me to brush my master's coat, but I refusing, a smart dialogue ensued, which ended in her bursting into tears of rage; when her mother interposing, and examining into the merits of the cause, determined it in my favor; and this good office I owed not to any esteem or

consideration she had for me, but solely to the
desire of mortifying her daughter, who on this
occasion observed, that let people be never so
much in the right, there were some folks who
would never do them justice; but, to be sure, they
had their reasons for it, which some people were
not ignorant of, although they despised their little
arts. This insinuation of *some people* and *some
folks,* put me upon observing the behavior of my
mistress more narrowly for the future; and it was
not long before I had reason to believe that she
looked upon her daughter as a rival in the af-
fections of Captain O'Donnell, who lodged in the
house. In the meantime, my industry and knowledge gained me the goodwill of my master, who
would often say in French, *"Mardie! c'est un bon
garçon."* He had a great deal of business; but
as he was mostly employed among his fellow-refu-
gees, his profits were small. However, his expense for medicines was not great, for he was
the most expert man at a succedaneum of any
apothecary in London; so that I have been sometimes amazed to see him, without the least hesitation, make up a physician's prescription, though
he had not in his shop one medicine mentioned in
it. Oyster-shells he could invent into crab's eyes;
common oil, into oil of sweet almonds; syrup of
sugar, into balsamic syrup; Thames water, into
aqua cinnamoni; turpentine, into capivi; and a
hundred more costly preparations were produced
in an instant, from the cheapest and coarsest
drugs of the *materia medica:* and when any common thing was ordered for a patient, he always

took care to disguise it in color or taste, or both,
in such a manner, as that it could not possibly
be known, for which purpose cochineal and oil
of cloves were of great service. Among many
nostrums which he possessed, there was one for
the venereal disease, that brought him a good
deal of money; and this he concealed so artfully
from me, that I could never learn its composition. But during the eight months I stayed in his
service, he was so unfortunate in the use of it,
that three parts in four of those who took it were
fain to confirm the cure by a salivation under the
direction of another doctor. This bad success, in
all appearance, attached him the more to his spe-
cific; and before I left him, I may venture to say,
he would have sooner renounced the Trinity, notwithstanding his being a good Huguenot, than his
confidence in the neverfailing power of this remedy. Mr. Lavement had attempted more than
once to introduce a vegetable diet into his family,
by launching out into the praise of roots and
greens, and decrying the use of flesh, both as a
physician and philosopher; but all his rhetoric
could not make one proselyte to his opinion; and
even the wife of his bosom declared against the
proposal. Whether it was owing to the little regard she paid to her husband's admonition in
this particular, or to the natural warmth of her
constitution, I know not; but this lady's passions
became every day more and more violent, till at
last she looked upon decency as an unnecessary
restraint; and one afternoon, when her husband
was abroad, and her daughter gone to visit, or-

dered me to call a hackney coach, in which she and the captain drove toward Covent Garden.

Miss came home in the evening, and, supping at her usual hour, went to bed. About eleven o'clock my master entered, and asked if his wife was gone to sleep; upon which I told him, my mistress went out in the afternoon, and was not yet returned. This was like a clap of thunder to the poor apothecary, who, starting back, cried, "*Mort de ma vie! vat you tell a me?* My wife not at home!" At that instant a patient's servant arrived with a prescription for a draught, which my master taking, went into the shop to make it up with his own hand. While he rubbed the ingredients in a glass mortar, he inquired of me, whether or not his wife went out alone; and no sooner heard that she was in company with the captain, than, with one blow, he split the mortar into a thousand pieces, and, grinning like the head of a bass viol, exclaimed, "Ah, traîtresse!" It would have been impossible for me to have preserved my gravity a minute longer, when I was happily relieved by a rap at the door, which I opened, and perceived my mistress coming out of the coach; she flounced immediately into the shop, and addressed her husband thus: "I suppose you thought I was lost, my dear—Captain O'Donnell has been so good as to treat me with a play." "Play, play," replied he, "oho! yes, by gar, I believe ver prettie play." "Bless me!" said she, "what's the matter?" "Vat de matter?" cried he, forgetting all his former complaisance, "by gar, you be one damn dog's wife—ventre bleu! me vill show you

vat it is to put one horn upon mine head. Per-
dieu! le Capitaine O'Donnell be one.''—Here the
captain, who had been all the while at the door
discharging the coach, entered, and said, with a
terrible voice, ''D—mme! what am I?'' Mr.
Lavement, changing his tone, immediately saluted
him with, *''Oh serviteur, Monsieur le Capitaine,
vous êtes un galant homme—ma femme est fort
obligée.''* Then, turning about toward me, pronounced with a low voice, *''Et diablement obli-
geante, sans doute.''* ''Harkee, Mr. Lavement,''
said the captain, ''I am a man of honor, and I believe you are too much of a gentleman to be offended at the civility I show your wife.''

This declaration had such an effect on the
apothecary, that he resumed all the politesse of a
Frenchman, and with the utmost prostration of
compliment, assured the captain that he was perfectly well satisfied with the honor he had done
his wife. Matters being thus composed, everybody went to rest. Next day, I perceived,
through a glass door that opened from the shop
into the parlor, the captain talking earnestly to
Miss, who heard him with a look that expressed
anger mingled with scorn; which, however, he at
last found means to mollify, and sealed his reconciliation with a kiss. This circumstance soon convinced me of the occasion of the quarrel; but
notwithstanding all my vigilance, I could never
discover any other commerce between them. In
the meanwhile, I had reason to believe I had inspired one of the maids with tender sentiments
for me; and one night, when I thought every

other person in the house asleep, I took the opportunity of going to reap the fruits of my conquest, her bedfellow having the day before gone to Richmond to visit her parents. Accordingly, I got up, and, naked as I was, explored my way in the dark to the garret where she lay. I was ravished to find the door open, and moved softly to her bedside, transported with the hope of completing my wishes. But what horrors of jealousy and disappointment did I feel, when I found her asleep, fast locked in the arms of a man, whom I easily guessed to be no other than the captain's servant! I was upon the point of doing some rash thing, when the noise of a rat scratching behind the wainscot put me to flight, and I was fain to get back to my own bed in safety. Whether this alarm had disordered my mind, or that I was led astray by the power of destiny, I know not; but, instead of turning to the left hand when I descended to the second story, I pursued the contrary course, and mistook the young lady's bedchamber for my own. I did not perceive my mistake before I had run against the bedposts, and then it was not in my power to retreat undiscovered; for the nymph being awake, felt my approach, and, with a soft voice, bade me make less noise, lest the Scotch booby in the next room should overhear us. This hint was sufficient to inform me of the nature of the assignation; and as my passions, at any time high, were then in a state of exaltation, I resolved to profit by my good fortune.

Without any more ceremony, therefore, I made

bold to slip into bed to this charmer, who gave me
as favorable a reception as I could desire. Our
conversation was very sparing on my part; but
she upbraided the person whom I represented
with his jealousy of me, whom she handled so
roughly, that my resentment had well-nigh occasioned a discovery more than once; but I was
consoled for her hatred of me by the revenge I
enjoyed in understanding from her own mouth
that it was now high time to salve her reputation
by matrimony; for she had reason to fear she
could not much longer conceal the effects of their
mutual intercourse. While I was meditating an
answer to this proposal, I heard a noise in my
room, like something heavy falling down upon the
floor; upon which I started up, and, creeping to
the door of my chamber, observed by moonlight
the shadow of a man groping his way out; so I
retired to one side to let him pass, and saw him
go downstairs as expeditiously as he could. It
was an easy matter to divine that this was the
captain, who, having overslept himself, had got up
at last to keep his assignation; and finding my
door open, had entered my apartment instead of
that of his mistress, where I supplied his place;
but finding his mistake, by falling over my chair,
he was afraid the noise might alarm the family,
and, for that reason, made off, delaying the gratification of his desires till another opportunity.
By this time I was satisfied; and, instead of returning to the place from whence I came, re-
treated to my own castle, which I fortified by bolt-

ing the door, and, in the congratulation of my own
happiness, fell asleep. But the truth of this adventure could not be long concealed from my
young mistress, who next day came to an explana-
tion with the captain, upon his lamenting his last
night's disappointment, and begging pardon for
the noise he had made. Their mutual chagrin,
when they came to the knowledge of what had
happened, may be easily conjectured, though each
had a peculiar grief unfelt by the other; for she
was conscious of not only having betrayed to me
the secrets of her commerce with him, but also of
having incensed me by the freedoms she had taken
with my name, beyond a hope of reconciliation.
On the other hand, his jealousy suggested that her
sorrow was all artifice, and that I had supplied
his place with her own privity and consent. That
such was the situation of their thoughts, will appear in the sequel; for that very day she came
into the shop where I was alone, and fixing her
eyes, swimming in tears, upon me, sighed most
piteously. But I was proof against her distress,
by recollecting the epithets with which she had
honored me the night before; and believing that
the good reception I enjoyed was destined for another, therefore I took no notice of her affliction;
and she had the mortification to find her disdain
returned fourfold. However, from thenceforward
she thought proper to use me with more complaisance than usual, knowing that it was in my power
at any time to publish her shame. By these
means my life became much more agreeable,

though I never could prevail upon myself to repeat my nocturnal visit; and, as I every day improved in my knowledge of the town, I shook off my awkward air by degrees, and acquired the character of a polite journeyman apothecary.

CHAPTER TWENTY

ONE night about twelve o'clock, as I returned from visiting a patient at Chelsea,
I received a blow on my head from an un-
seen hand, that stretched me senseless on the
ground; and was left for dead, with three stabs
of a sword in my body. The groans I uttered,
when I recovered the use of my reason, alarmed
the people of a solitary alehouse that stood near
the spot where I lay, and they were humane
enough to take me in, and send for a surgeon,
who dressed my wounds, and assured me they
were not mortal. One of them penetrated through
the skin and muscles of one side of my belly in
such a manner, that doubtless the assassin imagined he had run me through the entrails. The
second slanted along one of my ribs; and the last,
which was intended for the finishing stroke, having been directed to my heart, the sword snapped
upon my breastbone, and the point remained sticking in the skin. When I reflected upon this event,
I could not persuade myself that I had been assaulted by a common footpad; because it is not

usual for such people to murder those they rob, especially when they meet with no resistance; and I found my money, and everything else about me (but my carcass) safe. I concluded, therefore, that I must either have been mistaken for another, or obliged to the private resentment of some secret enemy for what had happened; and as I could remember nobody who had the least cause of complaint against me, except Captain O'Donnell and my master's daughter, my suspicion settled upon them, though I took care to conceal it, that I might the sooner arrive at confirmation.

With this view, I went home in a chair about ten o'clock in the morning; and as the chairman supported me into the house, met the captain in the passage, who no sooner saw me, than he started back, and gave evident signs of guilty confusion, which he would have accounted for from the surprise occasioned by seeing me in such a condition. My master having heard my story, condoled me with a good deal of sympathy, and when he understood my wounds were not dangerous, ordered me to be carried upstairs to bed; though not without some opposition from his wife, who was of opinion, it would be better for me to go to an hospital, where I should be more carefully attended. My meditation was employed in concerting with myself some method of revenge against Squire O'Donnell and his inamorata, whom I looked upon as the authors of my misfortune; when Miss (who was not at home at my arrival) entered my chamber, and, saying she was sorry for the accident that had befallen me, asked if I

suspected anybody to be the assassin: upon which
I fixed my eyes steadfastly upon her, and answered, "Yes." She discovered no symptom of
confusion; but replied hastily, "If that be the
case, why don't you take out a warrant to have
him apprehended? It will cost but a trifle; if you
have no money, I'll lend you." This frankness
not only cured me of my suspicion with respect to
her; but even staggered my belief with regard to
the captain, of whose guilt I resolved to have further proof before I should enterprise anything
in the way of revenge.

I thanked her kindly for her generous offer;
which, however, I had no occasion to accept, being determined to do nothing rashly: for though
I could plainly perceive the person who attacked
me to be a soldier, whose face I thought was familiar to me, I could not swear with a safe conscience to any particular man; and, granting I
could, my prosecution of him would not much
avail. This uncertainty I pretended, lest the captain, hearing from her that I knew the person
who wounded me, might think proper to withdraw
before I could be in a condition to requite him.
In two days I was up, and able to do a little
business, so that Mr. Lavement made shift to
carry on his practice, without hiring another journeyman in my room. The first thing I attempted
toward a certain discovery of my secret enemy,
was to get into O'Donnell's apartment while he
was abroad in an undress, and examine his sword,
the point of which being broken off, I applied the
fragment that was found sticking in my body, and

found it answered the fractured part exactly.
There was no room left for doubt; and all that
remained was to fix upon a scheme of revenge,
which almost solely engrossed my thoughts during the space of eight nights and days. Sometimes I was tempted to fall upon him in the same
manner as he had practiced upon me, and kill him
outright. But this assault my honor opposed as a
piece of barbarous cowardice, in which he was not
to be imitated. At other times I entertained
thoughts of demanding satisfaction in an honor-
able way; but was diverted from this undertaking by considering the uncertainty of the event,
and the nature of the injury he had done me,
which did not entitled him to such easy terms.
At last I determined to pursue a middle course;
and actually put my design in execution after
this manner. Having secured the assistance of
Strap and two of his acquaintances whom he could
depend upon, we provided ourselves with disguises, and I caused the following letter to be delivered to him by one of our associates in livery
one Sunday evening:—

"SIR,—If I may be allowed to judge from appearance, it
will not be disagreeable to you to hear that my husband is
gone to Bagshot to visit a patient, and will not return till
to-morrow night; so that if you have anything to propose
to me (as your behavior on many occasions has seemed to
insinuate), you will do well to embrace the present opportunity of seeing   Yours, etc."

This letter was signed with the name of an
apothecary's wife who lived in Chelsea, of whom

I had heard O'Donnell was an admirer. Everything succeeded to our wish. The amorous hero hastened toward the place of assignation; and was encountered by us in the very place where he had assaulted me. We rushed upon him all at once, secured his sword, stripped off his clothes even to the skin, which we scourged with nettles till he was blistered from head to foot, notwithstanding all the eloquence of his tears and supplications.

When I was satisfied with the stripes I had bestowed, we carried off his clothes, which we hid in a hedge near the place, and left him stark naked to find his way home in the best manner he could, while I took care to be there before him. I afterward understood, that, in his way to the lodgings of a friend who lived in the skirts of the town, he was picked up by the watch, who carried him to the Round House, from whence he sent for clothes to his lodgings; and next morning arrived at the door in a chair, wrapped up in a blanket he had borrowed; for his body was so sore and swelled, that he could not bear to be confined in his wearing apparel. He was treated with the utmost tenderness by my mistress and her daughter, who vied with each other in their care and attendance of him; but Lavement himself could not forbear expressing his joy, by several malicious grins, while he ordered me to prepare an unguent for his sores. As to myself, nobody can doubt my gratification when I had every day an opportunity of seeing my revenge protracted on the body of my adversary, by the ulcers of which I had been the cause; and indeed I not only enjoyed the satisfaction of having flayed him alive, but another also which I had not foreseen. The story of his being attacked and stripped in such a place having been inserted in the news, gave information to those who found his clothes next day whither to bring them; and accordingly he retrieved everything he had lost, except a few letters, among which was that which I had writ to him in the name of the apothecary's wife. This and the others, which, it seems, were all on the subject of love (for this Hibernian hero was one of those people who are called fortune-hunters), fell into the hands of a certain female author, famous for the scandal she has published, who, after having embellished them with some ornaments of her own invention, gave them to the town in print.

I was very much shocked on reflecting, that I might possibly be the occasion of a whole family's unhappiness, on account of the letter I had written; but was eased of that apprehension, when I understood that the Chelsea apothecary had commenced a law-suit against the printer for defamation; and looked upon the whole as a piece of forgery committed by the author, who had disappeared. But whatever might be his opinion of the matter, our two ladies seemed to entertain a different idea of it: for, as soon as the pamphlet appeared, I could perceive their care of their patient considerably diminish, until at last it ended in total neglect. It was impossible for him to be ignorant of this change, any more than of the oc-

casion of it; but as he was conscious to himself
of having deserved worse than contempt at their
hands, he was glad to come off so cheaply, and
contented himself with muttering curses and
threats against the apothecary, who, as he imagined, having got an inkling of the appointment
with his wife, had taken revenge of him in the
manner described. By the time he got a new scarf
skin, his character was become so notorious, that
he thought it high time for him to decamp; and
his retreat he performed in one night without beat
of drum, after having robbed his own servant of
everything that belonged to him, except the
clothes he had on his back. A few days after he
had disappeared, Mr. Lavement, for his own security, took into custody a large old trunk which
he had left; and, as it was very heavy, made no
question that the contents were sufficient to in-
demnify him for what O'Donnell owed in lodging.
But a month being elapsed without hearing any
tidings of this adventurer, and my master being
impatient to know what the trunk contained, he
ordered me to break it open in his presence,
which task I performed with the pestle of our
great mortar, and discovered, to his inexpressible astonishment and mortification, a heap of
stones.

About this time my friend Strap informed me
of an offer he had to go abroad with a gentleman,
in quality of valet-de-chambre, and at the same
time assured me, that whatever advantage he
might propose to himself from this prospect, he
could not bear the thoughts of parting from me;

so much was he attached to my fortune. In spite
of all the obligations I owed to this poor honest
fellow, ingratitude is so natural to the heart of
man, that I began to be tired of his acquaintance;
and now that I had contracted other friendships
which appeared more creditable, was even
ashamed to see a journeyman barber inquiring
after me with the familiarity of a companion. I
therefore, on pretense of consulting his welfare,
insisted upon his accepting the proposal, which
he at last determined to embrace with great re-
luctance; and in a few days took his leave of me,
shedding a flood of tears, which I could not be-
hold without emotion. I now began to look upon
myself as a gentleman in reality—learned to
dance of a Frenchman whom I had cured of a
fashionable distemper—frequented plays during
the holidays—became the oracle of an alehouse,
where every dispute was referred to my decision
—and at length contracted an acquaintance with
a young lady, who found means to make a conquest of my heart, and upon whom I prevailed,
after much attendance and solicitation, to give me
a promise of marriage. As this beautiful creature
passed for a rich heiress, I blessed my good fortune, and was actually on the point of crowning
all my wishes by matrimony; when one morning
I went to her lodgings, and her maid being abroad,
took the privilege of a bridegroom to enter her
chamber, where, to my utter confusion, I found
her in bed with a man. Heaven gave me patience
and presence of mind enough to withdraw imme-

diately; and I thanked my stars a thousand times for the happy discovery, by which I resolved to profit so much as to abandon all thoughts of marriage for the future.

CHAPTER TWENTY-ONE

Squire Gawky comes to lodge with my Master—Is involved
in a troublesome Affair, out of which he is extricated
by me—He marries my Master's Daughter—They conspire against me—I am found guilty of Theft—Discharged—Deserted by my Friends—I hire a Room in St.
Giles's—Where, by accident, I find the Lady to whom
I made my Addresses in a miserable Condition—I relieve
her.

WHILE I enjoyed myself at large in this
temper of mind, Mr. Lavement let his
first floor to my countryman and acquaintance, Squire Gawky, who, by this time, had
got a lieutenancy in the army, and such a martial
ferocity in his appearance, that I was afraid he
would remember what had happened between us
in Scotland, and atone for his breach of appointment then, by his punctuality now; but, whether
he had actually forgot me, or was willing to make
me believe so, he betrayed not the least symptom
of recognition at sight of me, and I remained
quite cured of my apprehension; though I had occasion, not long after, to be convinced that, how-
soever his externals might be altered, he was at
bottom the same individual Gawky whom I have
already described. For, coming home late one
night from the house of a patient, I heard a noise
in the street, and, as I approached, perceived two
gentlemen in custody of three watchmen.

The prisoners, who were miserably disfigured with dirt, complained bitterly of the loss of their hats and wigs; and one of them, whom, by his tongue, I knew to be a Scotchman, lamented most piteously, offering a guinea for his liberty, which the watchman refused, alleging that one of his companions was wounded grievously, and that he must stand to the consequence. My prejudice in favor of my country was so strong, that I could not bear to see anybody belonging to it in distress, and therefore, with one blow of my faithful cudgel, knocked down the watchman who had hold of the person for whom I was chiefly concerned. He was no sooner disengaged, than he betook himself to his heels, and left me to maintain the dispute as I should think proper; and, indeed, I came off but scurvily; for, before I could avail myself of my speed, I received a blow on the eye from one of the other two, that had well-nigh deprived me of the use of that organ. However, I made shift to get home, where I was informed of Captain Gawky's being robbed and abused by a company of footpads, and was ordered by my master to prepare an emollient glyster and paregoric draught, in order to allay and compose the ferment of his spirits, occasioned by the barbarous treatment he had undergone, while he took twelve ounces of blood from him immediately. When I inquired into the particulars of this adventure, and understood, by the servant, that he came in just before me, without hat and wig, I made no scruple of believing him to be the person I had released, and was confirmed in my belief upon hearing his voice, to which, before that event, I had been so long a stranger. My eyes being considerably swelled and inflamed, I could not reflect upon my enterprise without cursing my own folly, and even resolving to declare the truth of the whole story, in order to be revenged on the cowardly wretch, for whom I had suffered. Accordingly, next day, after he had told, in the presence of my master, his wife, and daughter, who came to visit him, a thousand lies concerning the prowess he had shown in making his escape, I ventured to explain the mystery, and, calling in the evidence of my contused eye, upbraided him with cowardice and ingratitude. Gawky was so astonished at this discourse, that he could not answer one word; and the rest of the company stared at one another; till, at length, my mistress reprimanded me for my insolent behavior, and threatened to turn me away for my presumption.

Upon which Gawky, having recollected himself, observed, as the young man might have mistaken another person for him, he could forgive his insinuations, more especially as he seemed to have suffered for his civility; but advised me to be more certain in my conjectures for the future, before I ventured to publish them to the prejudice of any man. Miss applauded the captain's generosity in pardoning one who had so villainously aspersed him, and I began to imagine her praise was not at all disinterested. But the apothecary, who, perhaps, had more penetration, or less partiality, than his wife and daughter, differed from them in his sentiments of the matter, and ex-

pressed himself to me in the shop in this manner: "Ah! mon pauvre Roderique! you ave more
of de véracité dan of de prudence—bot mine vife
and dater be diablement sage, and Mons. le Capitaine un fanfaron, pardieu!" This eulogium on
his wife and daughter, though spoken ironically
by him, was, nevertheless, literally just; by es-
pousing the cause of Gawky, the one obliged a
valuable lodger, and the other acquired a husband at a juncture when one was absolutely necessary; for the young lady, finding the effects òf her
correspondence with O'Donnell becoming plainer
and plainer every day, insinuated herself so artfully into the affection of this new lodger, that in
less than a fortnight, on pretense of going to a
play, they drove away together to the Fleet, where
they were coupled; from thence removed to a bag-
nio, where the marriage was consummated; and in
the morning came home, where they asked her
father's and mother's blessing. The prudent
parents, notwithstanding the precipitation with
which the match was carried on, did not think fit
to refuse their approbation; for the apothecary
was not ill pleased to find his daughter married to
a young man of a good prospect, who had not
mentioned to him one syllable on the article of her
dowry; and his wife was rejoiced at being rid of
a rival in her gallants, and a spy upon her pleasures. Nor was I without self-enjoyment at this
event, when I reflected upon the revenge I had un-
wittingly taken upon my enemy, in making him a
cuckold by anticipation. But I little dreamed
what a storm of mischief was brewing against me,

whilst I thus indulged myself. Whatever face
Gawky put on the matter, my discovery of the adventure before related, and the reproaches I
vented against him, had stung him to the soul, and
cherished the seeds of enmity so strongly in his
breast, that he, it seems, imparted his indignation to his wife, who being as desirous as himself
to compass the ruin of one that not only slighted
her caresses, but was able on any occasion to discover particulars not at all advantageous to her
character, readily joined in a conspiracy against
me, which, had it taken effect as they expected,
would infallibly have brought me to an ignomin-
ious death.

My master having several times missed large
quantities of medicines, of which I could give no
account, at last lost all patience, and, in plain
terms, taxed me with having embezzled them for
my own use. As I could only oppose my single
asseveration to his suspicion, he told me one day,
"By gar, your vord not be give me de satisfaction—me find necessaire to chercher for my medicine, pardonnez-moi—il faut chercher—me demand le clef of your coffre a cette heure." Then
raising his voice to conceal the fright he was in,
lest I should make any opposition, he went on,
"Oui, foutre, I charge you rendez le clef of your
coffre—moi—si, moi qui vous parle." I was fired
with so much resentment and disdain at this ac-
cusation, that I burst into tears, which he took
for a sign of my guilt; and, pulling out my key,
told him he might satisfy himself immediately,
though he would not find it so easy to satisfy me

for the injury my reputation had suffered from his unjust suspicion. He took the key, and mounted up to my chamber, attended by the whole family; saying, "Hé bien, nous verrons—nous verrons." But what was my horror and amazement, when, on opening my chest, he pulled out a handful of the very things that were missing, and pronounced, "Ah ha! vous êtes bien venus—mardie, Mons. Roderique, you be fort innocent."

I had not power to utter one word in my own vindication, but stood motionless and silent, while everybody present made their respective remarks on what appeared against me. The servants said they were sorry for my misfortune, and went away repeating, "Who would have thought it?" My mistress took occasion, from this detection, to rail against the practice of employing strangers in general; and Mrs. Gawky, after having observed that she never had a good opinion of my fidelity, proposed to have me carried before a justice, and committed to Newgate immediately. Her husband was actually upon the stairs in his way for a constable, when Mr. Lavement, knowing the cost and trouble of a prosecution to which he must bind himself, and at the same time dreading lest some particlars of my confession might affect his practice, called out, "Restez, mon fils! restez, it be véritablement one grand crime which dis pauvre diable have committed—bot peutêtre de good God give him de penitence, and we vill not have upon mine head de blood of one sinner." The captain and his lady used all the Christian arguments their zeal could suggest, to prevail on

the apothecary to pursue me to destruction, and
represented the injustice he did to the community
of which he was a member, in letting a villain escape, who would not fail of doing more mischief
in the world, when he should reflect on his coming
off so easily now. But their eloquence made no
impression on my master, who, turning to me,
said, ''Go, miserable, go from mine house, quick,
quick—and make reparation for your mauvaise
actions.''

By this time my indignation had roused me
from the stupefaction in which I had hitherto remained, and I began in this manner: ''Sir, appearances, I own, condemn me; but you are imposed upon as much as I am abused. I have fallen a sacrifice to the rancor of that scoundrel,''
pointing to Gawky, ''who has found means to
convey your goods hither, that the detection of
them might blast my reputation, and accomplish
my destruction. His hatred of me is owing to a
consciousness of his having wronged me in my
own country; for which injury he, in a cowardly
manner, refused me the satisfaction of a gentleman. He knows, moreover, that I am no stranger
to his dastardly behavior in this town, which I
have recounted before; and he is unwilling that
such a testimony of his ingratitude and pusillan-
imity should live upon the earth. For this reason
he is guilty of the most infernal malice to bring
about my ruin. And I am afraid, madam,'' turning to Mrs. Gawky, ''you have too easily entered
into the sentiments of your husband. I have
often found you my enemy, and am well ac-

quainted with the occasion of your being so, which
I don't at present think proper to declare; but I
would not advise you, for your own sake, to
drive me to extremity." This address enraged
her so much, that, with a face as red as scarlet,
and the eyes of a fury, she strutted up to me, and,
putting her hands on her sides, spit in my face,
saying I was a scandalous villain, but she defied
my malice; and that, unless her papa would prosecute me like a thief as I was, she would not stay
another night under his roof. At the same time
Gawky, assuming a big look, told me he scorned
what lies I could invent against him! but that,
if I pretended to asperse his wife, he would put
me to death, by G—d. To this threat I answered,
"I wish to God I could meet with thee in a desert,
that I might have an opportunity of punishing
thee for thy perfidy toward me, and rid the world
of such a rascal. What hinders me this moment," said I, seizing an old bottle that stood by,
"from doing myself that justice?" I had no
sooner armed myself in this manner, than Gawky
and his father-in-law retired in such a hurry, that
the one overturned the other, and they rolled together downstairs; while my mistress swooned
away with fear; and her daughter asked if I intended to murder her? I gave her to understand,
that nothing was further from my intention; that
I would leave her to the stings of her own conscience, but was firmly resolved to slit her husband's nose, whenever fortune should offer a con-
venient opportunity.

Then going downstairs, I met Lavement coming

up trembling with the pestle in his hand, and Gawky behind, armed with his sword, pushing him forward. I demanded a parley, and having assured them of my pacific disposition, Gawky exclaimed, "Ah! villain! you have killed my dear wife." And the apothecary cried, "Ah, coquin! vere is my shild?" "The lady," said I, "is above stairs, unhurt by me, and will a few months hence, I believe, reward your concern." Here she called to them, and desired they would let the wretch go, and trouble themselves no further about him. To which request her father consented, observing, nevertheless, that my conversation was fort mystérieuse. Finding it impossible to vindicate my innocence, I left the house immediately, and went to the schoolmaster, with an intention of clearing myself to him, and asking his advice with regard to my future conduct; but, to my inexpressible vexation, was told he was gone to the country, where he would stay two or three days. I returned with a design of consulting some acquaintances I had acquired in my master's neighborhood; but my story had taken air, through the officiousness of the servants, and not one of my friends would vouchsafe me a hearing. Thus I found myself, by the iniquity of mankind, in a much more deplorable condition than ever: for though I had been formerly as poor, my reputation was without blemish, and my health unimpaired till now; but at present my good name was lost, my money gone, my friends were alienated, my body was infected by a distemper contracted in the course of an amour, and my faithful Strap, who alone could yield me pity and assistance, absent I knew not where.

The first resolution I could take in this melancholy conjuncture, was to remove my clothes to the house of the person with whom I had formerly lodged, where I remained two days, in hopes of getting another place, by the interest of Mr. Concordance, to whom I made no doubt of being able to vindicate my character; but in this supposition I reckoned without my host, for Lavement took care to be beforehand with me, and when I attempted to explain the whole affair to the schoolmaster, I found him so prepossessed against me, that he would scarce hear me to an end; but when I had finished my justification, shook his head, and beginning with his usual exclamation, "O Ch—st!" said, "That won't go down with me. I am very sorry I should have the misfortune of being concerned in the affair, but, however, shall be more cautious for the future. I will trust no man from henceforward— no, not my father who begat me—nor the brother who lay with me in my mother's womb. Should Daniel rise from the dead, I would think him an impostor, and were the genius of Truth to appear, would question its veracity." I told him, that one day it was possible he might be convinced of the injury I had suffered, and repent of his premature determination. To which remark he answered, the proof of my innocence would make his bowels to vibrate with joy; "but till that shall happen," continued he, "I must beg to have no manner of connection with you—

my reputation is at stake—O my good God! I shall
be looked upon as your accomplice and abettor—
people will say Jonathan Wild was but a type
of me—boys will hoot at me as I pass along, and
the cinder-wenches belch forth reproaches wafted
in a gale impregnated with gin—I shall be notorious—the very butt of slander and cloak of
infamy.'' I was not in a humor to relish the cli-
max of expressions upon which this gentleman
valued himself in all his discourses; but, without
any ceremony, took my leave, cursed with every
sentiment of horror which my situation could suggest. I considered, however, in the intervals of
my despondence, that I must in some shape suit
my expense to my calamitous circumstances; and
with that view hired an apartment in a garret
near St. Giles's, at the rate of ninepence per week.
In this place I resolved to perform my own cure,
having first pawned three shirts to purchase medicines and support for the occasion.

One day when I sat in this solitary retreat, mus-
ing upon the unhappiness of my fate, I was
alarmed by a groan that issued from a chamber
contiguous to mine, into which I immediately ran,
and found a woman stretched on a miserable
truckle bed, without any visible signs of life.
Having applied a smelling bottle to her nose, the
blood began to revisit her cheeks, and she opened
her eyes; but, good heavens! what were the emo-
tions of my soul, when I discovered her to be the
same individual lady who had triumphed over
my heart, and to whose fate I had almost been
inseparably joined! Her deplorable situation

filled my breast with compassion, and every tender idea reviving in my imagination, I flew into
her embrace. She knew me immediately; and,
straining me gently in her arms, shed a torrent
of tears, which I could not help increasing. At
length, casting a languishing look at me, she pronounced, with a feeble voice, "Dear Mr. Random,
I do not deserve this concern at your hands. I
am a vile creature who had a base design upon
your person; suffer me to expiate that and all my
other crimes by a miserable death, which will not
fail to overtake me in a few hours." I encouraged her as much as I could; told her I forgave
all her intentions with regard to me; and that,
although my circumstances were extremely low,
I would share my last farthing with her. In the
meantime, begged to know the immediate cause
of that fit from which she had just recovered, and
said, I would endeavor by my skill to prevent any
more such attacks. She seemed very much affected with this expression, took my hand and
pressed it to her lips, saying, "You are too generous!—I wish I could live to express my grati-
tude; but alas! I perish for want." Then, shut-
ting her eyes, she relapsed into another swoon.
Such extremity of distress must have awakened
the most obdurate heart to sympathy and compassion. What effect, then, must it have had on
mine, that was naturally prone to every tender
passion? I ran downstairs, and sent my landlady
to a chemist's shop for some cinnamon water;
while I, returning to this unfortunate creature's
chamber, used all the means in my power to bring

her to herself. This aim, with much difficulty, I accomplished, and made her drink a glass of the cordial to recruit her spirits; then I prepared a little mulled red wine and a toast, which having taken, she found herself thoroughly revived, and informed me, that she had not tasted food for eight-and-forty hours before. As I was impatient to know the occasion and nature of her calamity, she gave me to understand, that she was a woman of the town by profession: that, in the course of her adventures, she found herself dangerously infected with a distemper to which all her class are particularly subject; that her malady gaining ground every day, she became loathsome to herself and offensive to others; when she resolved to retire to some obscure corner, where she might be cured with as little noise and expense as possible; that she had accordingly chosen this place of retreat, and put herself into the hands of an advertising doctor, who having fleeced her of all the money she had, or could procure, left her three days ago in a worse condition than that in which he found her: that, except the clothes on her back, she had pawned or sold everything that belonged to her, to satisfy that rapacious quack, and quiet the clamor of her landlady, who still persisted in her threats to turn her out into the street.

After having moralized upon these particulars, I proposed that she should lodge in the same room with me, an expedient that would save some money; and assured her I would undertake her cure as well as my own, during which she should partake of all the conveniences that I could afford to myself. She embraced my offer with unfeigned acknowledgment; and I began to put it in practice immediately. I found in her not only an agreeable companion, whose conversation greatly alleviated my chagrin, but also a careful nurse, who served me with the utmost fidelity and affection. One day, while I testified my surprise that a woman of her beauty, good sense, and education (for she had a large portion of each), could be reduced to such an infamous and miserable way of life as that of a prostitute,—she answered, with a sigh, "These very advantages were the cause of my undoing." This remarkable reply inflamed my curiosity to such a degree, that I begged she would favor me with the particulars of her story, and she complied in these words:—

END OF VOL. I.